VALENCIES

VALENCIES

A SCIENCE FICTION NOVEL

DAMIEN BRODERICK

& RORY BARNES

THE BORGO PRESS

MMXIII

VALENCIES

FIRST BORGO PRESS EDITION

Published by Wildside Press LLC

www.wildsidebooks.com

DEDICATION

For the Magic Realists of Lot 4, Wellington Road: Chris, Delwyn, Di, Helene, Jean, Jill, John, Jon, Phillip, Ponch, Sandy, Tony, Val

CONTENTS

PREFACE 2013

Valencies was first published in 1983 by the University of Queensland Press, St. Lucia, Queensland, Australia and this edition is slightly revised and extended. It deals with an episode in a long, long face-off between repression and freedom, a future where everyone is immune to aging yet entire stars can be blown up to destroy rebels against an empire linked by teleport gates throughout the galaxy (and you have to go through them naked). It's about strangers in a very strange land finding love. But it's not a military adventure yarn nor a romance in deep space. What is it, then?

In *The Penguin New Literary History of Australia*, science fiction critic Professor Van Ikin commented: "[U]topia is an elusive grail with a different meaning in every age, and contemporary writers of speculative fiction...examine the dangers and pitfalls of utopian fervour. The most notable of these works are *Beloved Son* (1978) and *Vaneglory* (1981) by George Turner, and *Valencies* (1983) by Rory Barnes and Damien Broderick." Critics Ikin, Dr. Sean McMullen, and Dr. Russell Blackford, in *Strange Constellations* (1999), also point out that "in its structure, although not its thematic concern with individual freedom and universal human dignity, the book is atypical of Broderick's fiction, quite different from his novels of time travel and altered realities...."

If all this sounds a little downbeat, take heart! Brian W. Aldiss, in his classic history of science fiction, *Trillion Year Spree*, praised *Valencies* as "one of the more playful SF novels of recent years" and quoted it at some length. Ikin, McMullen, and Blackford say: "Some of the book's set pieces...are glorious pieces of comic writing." So, yes, it is a literary dystopia, but we hope it's a lot of fun as well.

In *Hyperdreams* (1998), Russell Blackford described the novel thus:

> A far-future parable about political and cultural imperialism. Barnes and Broderick propose that by 4004 AD the Universe has been filled with human beings, thanks to the teleportational network (the "Aorist Discontinuity") and countless terraformed planets left behind by a von Danikenesque alien race known as "the Charioteers." Humanity is organised into a bleak and clinically brutal Empire. The novel focuses on a frustrated group of libertarian anarchists who live on the planet Victoria. By the end, their politically futile activities elicit from the reader a mixed emotional response. There is a sense of pathos, since all the moves in the game are foreknown and controlled by the rulers of the Empire, as becomes apparent in the final chapter, while the book's revolutionaries cannot even understand each other, let alone overthrow an omnipotently entrenched system. At the same time, there is a strong sense of dignity and courage, and this is magnified rather than diminished by the depictions of human weakness. *Valencies*, then, represents a struggle against Empire, a struggle that can never amount to more than futile gestures. The narrative is dominated by the characters' pranks, games, and parodies, and the complexities of their love lives. The incomprehension between person and person is suggested not only by the book's focus upon the difficulties between spirited Anla and dispirited Ben, and those between vulnerable Theri and gentle Kael, but also by the cunning

juxtaposition of narrative viewpoints, which enables Barnes and Broderick to weave for the reader a delicate web of understanding of the characters' misunderstandings.

If this is (like much science fiction) a relic of a future that never happened—sadly, for example, the Good Doctor Isaac Asimov is no longer alive in this real tomorrow—we're quite content to note that in one respect we saw farther than our critics in the early 1980s. One of them denounced us for our failure of imagination in supposing that students and other radical activists would in future gather once more in the streets and parks to confront the rich, the powerful and the brutal. *So 1960s!* we were told dismissively. Then the massacre of student protesters in China's Tiananmen Square shocked the rest of the world in 1989, and the Berlin Wall fell before the fury of those sickened finally by the gulag cultures, and later the Occupy movement took to the streets of the USA, and the Arab Spring changed the Middle East tyrannies, or tried to, and not all of it was hopeless and self-deluding.

So we don't expect the real future to be much like the setting of *Valencies*, but we're pretty sure that generation after generation will keep finding ways (sometimes with sarcastic laughter) to confront the absolute power that inevitably corrupts everyone who wields it.

—Damien Broderick
Rory Barnes
March 2013

Our babes'll wander naked
through the Cities of the Universe.
Blows Against the Empire
Jefferson Airplane

The strangers of the Foundation knew nothing of the swirling days and nights of the bloody Sack that had left the University untouched. They knew nothing of the time after the collapse of the Imperial power, when the students, with their borrowed weapons, and their pale-faced inexperienced bravery, formed a protective volunteer army to protect the central shrine of the science of the Galaxy.

Foundation and Empire
Isaac Asimov

PART ONE

1.

He was two thousand years from home, lonely as only the ancient can be lonely, sick at heart.

"Matey," he called to the lout murdering the guitar at the next table, "lend us your axe for a mo?"

The fellow gave him a contemptuous glance, smacked his fingers clumsily against the strings. Catsize leaned forward on his timber table-top, expectant, undeterred. One of the young women at the other table glanced back over her shoulder.

"You play?"

"Bit." He shrugged. "You know."

"My gran made this with his own bare hands," the lout said resentfully. He placed the guitar on the table in front of him. Red and green glistened from the veneer, caught the scratches in its polish.

"It's a beauty," Catsize agreed. He left his arms folded. "You play it real good, zinger."

The fellow's lips twisted. "Yeah, well, it's a hobby of mine. The fuckin' imperials don't like it, see?"

Catsize was impressed, widening his eyes in the dim light of the swig bar. "You know any...seditious songs?"

Now all of them were looking at him, hard and suspicious. He gazed from one to the other, mild, slightly dopey, and saw them relax.

"Give him a go, Scums."

"Bit of a laugh, anyway."

The big fellow hesitated, then abruptly shrugged and thrust the instrument across the gap between them. "Treat it with respect, zotter. My gran—"

"Made it, yeah." Catsize hefted it. Not too bad, balance was okay. He tightened the strings. Clear notes rang like ice.

"Sing us one of those songs. You know," the interested woman said.

"Well, okay." With a last quaff from his jar, Catsize sounded a run of notes that turned every head in the bar. "This is a real old one, I'm told. From some place so far away you need to take a hundred Aorist trips to get here." He sang, then, in his cracked, angelic voice:

> "'Twas brillig, and the slithy toves
> "Did gyre and gimble in the wabe;
> "All mimsy were the borogoves—"

When he came up for air, exultant and flushed with the joy of it, they clicked their fingers, and someone on the far side of the bar hooted in approval.

"Cool, man." The lout was impressed. "Was that about...?" Scums lowered his voice, looked around furtively. "Kurd?"

Catsize gave him a knowing look.

"What's it mean, man?" the woman asked. She left her bench at the other table, came to sit beside him.

"It's Creole," he told her. "Man probably shouldn't, you know...."

"No," she said, nodding, then shook her head. "No."

"Sing us something else, zinger."

"Aw."

"Go on."

"My throat's dry."

"Get the guy a drink, Marty."

Catsize leaned back, the large bulk of the antique instrument fitting against his body like a lover.

"This is a dude from Old Earth. Yeats." He closed his eyes and sang:

> *Under the passing stars*
> *Foam of the sky*
> *Lives on this lonely face—*

As he drew to the end of the ancient ballad, tears leaked from his meshed lashes.

Finally he handed back the guitar, head ringing, fingers numb. He went to the lavatory out back, under the white fragrance of some mutant vegetable from earth, the scent of salt and kelp, listening to the sound of the ocean beyond the pub's high walls, and when he came out into the night the woman was waiting for him. She took his arm and drew him into deeper shadow. Voices played like mantras within the bar, enriched with bursts of laughter. He allowed himself to follow her into shadow. She kissed him, deeply, like a besotted girl, placing his right hand on her full breast. For the first time in years he felt aroused. She pulled away, then.

"They want you back, Commander."

He sighed. She was beautiful, but they were all beautiful now.

"We've been looking for you for a very long time."

He found a waist-high garbage container, hopped up on it, the painted metal chilly under his buttocks, and pulled the woman close to him. Into her ear he said, "Chomsky is closed."

"Yes. Interdicted. But we won't stay closed forever, Commander."

"Open the gates again and the Imperials will be all over us like swarming rats."

"Not if those of us on the outside do our jobs."

"The Revolution, ah yes." Catsize sighed. A perfumed Newstralian wind blew across the buzz garden, and the sea hushed and retreated. The woman leaned back against him, solid, alive, yes, still somehow alive.

"You are sardonic, sir." Her voice came crisp through the

haze of her long hair. She turned her face sideways, to him, allowing any spy who chanced to be watching them to assume a kiss. "But yes, the revolution. We need you back with us."

Two thousand years blew through his small body like stale incinerator smoke.

"I find it cold out here, my dear. My poor old bones, you know." Catsize kept his hands on her for balance and for the memory of it, pushed himself down off the trash container. His feet crunched in sand. She was a good head taller, her hair in his lips. "I'm expecting some friends. It was pleasant to meet you."

"Sir—"

"Tell them I fought the good fight. Tell them I'm retired." In the half light, Catsize rubbed his aching eyes with the heels of his hands, then smiled up at her. "No, nobody would believe that. Tell them I have my own way of doing things."

The woman's mouth twisted. "Commander, I'm disappointed. We've been searching for you for more than century. Am I supposed to report that you've become nothing better than an...adventurist?"

"Tell them that I wish them well, as always." He reached up, drew her down in an embrace, kissed her lowered forehead as one might kiss a child's head, a child one loves, a child one must leave now. "Tell them— Well, you could tell them that the mome rath outgrabe."

"The— Sir, what the *fuck* does that mean?"

He beamed at her, delighted. "There, I *knew* you were an anarchist at heart. 'Sir', indeed. Good grief." He bowed. "Good evening, and farewell," and took himself back to the thick fuggy air of the swig. Kael and Theri had arrived. They waved, beckoned him to a table. Through the heavy timber doors from the dropspace out front, Ben and Anla entered, arguing ferociously. Catsize beamed. His children. His wonderful innocents.

"Drinks!" he cried to them, capering. "Buzz! Poetry and song!"

Everyone smiled.

2.

"Banal tinkering?" Putting his spasm of outrage to best advantage, the DNA sculptor indolently slipped lower on his couch. "Surely you're confusing my profession with the vulgar craft of cosmetic genetics."

Anla lifted one knee a trifle. Recklessly, the sculptor told her, "Why, if it weren't for our work the entire logistics of Empire would be inconceivable, you silly, pretty little foddle."

Instead of punching him on the nose, Anla clapped her thighs together, skidding him down the spine of a snake to totter dismayed at the foot of a ladder he'd begun to ascend an hour earlier.

"I've picked up a fact or two during my meager span, doctor," she said. "I certainly don't want a lecture on gene promoters and repressors at this point in the evening. It's the tune your fiddling produces that I object to."

"But now I've offended you!" Reluctantly he sat higher and seized her hand. "There's no call for formality. Ralf's my name and you must use it, for I'm sure we're meant to be firm friends."

"What, a man of your considerable caliber interested in a silly little female, a funny wee muffin, a fluff-brained baby chicken, a double-X chromosomed foddle, a twat—"

"My dear, of course it was a clumsy thing to say and I do apologize. I acknowledge your intelligence. I like women. But you happen to be mistaken about stochastic biosis."

Smiling faintly, Anla uncrossed her legs, and allowed her knees to begin once more their slow tectonic drift. "Suppose we give politics a miss," she said, with every semblance of conciliation. "No doubt you deem my views puerile, as I consider yours senile."

A hovering toff, resplendent in codpiece and chiffon, threw himself down beside her and let his dark hand fall on her bare calf. "Oh I say, my sweet, that's rather unsporting. I've known Ralf since he was a babe in arms. He's no older than your father."

"I haven't got a father."

"Oh." The toff blinked. "You're a clone?"

"No, they found me under a cabbage patch. Of course I'm a clone."

"I'm sure we didn't mean to put you in a state. Can I get you a stimulant?"

"How kind." Most of the gathering had subsided to the floor, or retired to privacy. Anla could spot none of her friends. As the toff glided away she caught a glimpse of her glowering husband, propped stiffly on the far side of the room. Bugger him, she thought irritably. What's wrong with the man, the place is crawling with it. Next to him swayed a bountiful woman of Dravidian extraction, eminently available, with a spangled cleavage as big as all outdoors. Thrust your hand in to the wrist, lad. You're supposed to be a tit man, aren't you? But all Ben did was scowl pitifully back at her before turning clumsily and shaking off the dust of his heels. Take that, you harlot. Oh shit, *toujours gai.*

A touch on her shoulder proved that the bloody toff had not been ambushed in the pursuit of his duties. Anla shot the stimulant buzz and ignored him in favor of Empire's manifest destiny.

"Ralf," she said, "did anyone ever tell you that you have beautiful eyes?"

§

"And just what do you propose doing when we've captured the little bugger?"

"Kill it," Kael said. "And then *eat* it."

"Hmm." Catsize brooded. "Killing it is just the kickoff. Then we've got to skin it and take out its guts."

"Half the inhabited universe once dined on meat," Kael said. "Our ancestors throve on it. You were there, Catsize, I'm sure you remember it well."

"All right." Catsize stood up. "You find the instrument, I'll bring the skite around." He nimbly hurdled outstretched, drunken legs, crossed the patio and jumped for the shadows; out and away, up the track to their hired skite. Kael went the other way, toward the kitchen.

Ben waited for them with Kael's Theri on the moonlit gravel, watching the waters of the river run black and well-polished between matched banks. Summer night, holiday world: dull gleam of vehicles, murmur of failing party. Only Anla's voice, precise and intelligent, rose distinctly, in debate with the gene-sculptor. And then the sculptor's laughter, overhearty, self-satisfied, across the blurred conversations of the other guests. Ben, surly, kicked at the gravel, pretending he hadn't heard.

They'd met the gene-sculptor in a waterside pub. He had bought Anla a buzz and put his arm around her shoulder, called her "my dear" and said he could tell by the karyotonic lines on her hand that she was impulsive and generous. An invitation to the party in the scrub had been issued with the second buzz, an invitation that could hardly exclude her friends—could hardly exclude, for that matter, her lawful bonded husband. Not that the sculptor could have inferred her unfashionably dyadic status: no antique sentimental ring constrained Anla's impulsive and generous hand.

Ben turned his back on the dim glow of the studio and the sound of his wife's familiar sexiness, stared at the reconstructed elms holding out their white arms to the travelling local moon. Celestial lair of foddles, safe under Imperial decree from human hands. He lowered his gaze and glared at what he saw. Fucking expensive, pretentious place. The bastard probably has a dacha like this on a hundred worlds, or a thousand. You can't take it with you, but you can find one just like it waiting at the other end if you're rich enough.

A neat peptide-schema on intergalactic monetary equivalents bounced up unsought into Ben's consciousness; he slapped it back down again. What must it be like after a thousand years of data inlays?

He squinted in the darkness. Granite and sandstone, ageless centenarians in doublets, their twittering girl crones, their toad-like sportskites cluttering up the dropspace. So low on the ground, some of these overpowered heaps of plast, that a well-aimed fusillade of gravel ends up on the webbing.

A fly-screen flared and Kael came silently from the dark end of the house, steel in his hand: a half meter of freshly sharpened carving knife. "What the hell are you up to?"

Ben, not bothering to reply, kicked another shower of gravel at a yellow coupe.

"He's just giving them a bit more ballistic ballast," Theri explained. "They need it for going round clouds."

"Ah."

The skite's light sliced down, made them blink. Kael and Theri clambered aboard and sorted themselves out astern. Ben slumped beside Catsize. The lift-field spurted gravel and the safari swung aloft, drive grumbling, lights tunneling across the mangy bush of the planet Newstralia. Bloody holidays.

§

Theri lay under the filament blanket, head on Kael's lap. The wind swirling over the open skite dried the sweat of the party from her face. Trees flickered below, branches webbing the soil. She wanted bed and sleep, not this midnight madness, this molesting of innocent foddles in the pastures of the night.

The whole exercise seemed slightly contrived, anyway. Kill an animal and eat it—the sort of jolly fantasy one floated at parties or during stoned evenings in pubs, not something one actually went out and did. Not someone like Kael, at least.

Probably he only pushed the plan along to get Ben out of the place. Give the lad something to do. Anla was obviously in no mood to leave her conversation with the gene-sculptor. So Kael hatched this absurd scheme, trying a little too hard to be carried away by the madcap spirit of the thing.

It was really only when Catsize decided to adopt the plan that it got off the ground. She thought: Poor old Kael's just slightly too rational, not quite manic enough for the exploit. She heard

Catsize endit the illegal program; he caught her eye and winked.

"Heads and elbows in," he said, and energized the bubble. "Going up."

§

The skite trudged up the gravity well, sliding a bit off its programmed trajectory, the corrugations of the geofield barely diminished by its rudimentary autonomics. Kael ran his hand under the blanket, found Theri's fingers and interlocked his own. The atmosphere ended and the skite bounced into open fields of clumpy stars, arctic in the night sky.

"I'd have thought that sanctuaries would be guarded," Ben said grumpily. "We'll never get through its operational envelope. We'll be arrested. Our loved ones will never hear of us again."

"I know a thing or two."

"You've been around, haven't you, Catsize," said Kael. "You've seen a thing or two that'd shock us."

"My oath."

"Catsize, how old are you?"

"Don't be obscene."

§

"You miss my point." The rowdy team of endorphins partying in Anla's brain-tissues were kicking up their heels and knocking the furniture about. Somehow this sportive chemical behavior had the effect of lengthening the room, giving everything she saw and heard a piercing clarity. Her amplified voice rang wearily down the enormous hall. "If we must go back to basics, what the hell do you find so glorious in the idea of Empire?"

The boring fellow was wrestling with his library. Much more on this tack and I might as well go home and fuck Ben. Chariots, look at it, though, he must be rolling in exchange-value. Thing's totally voice-activated, not a key on it.

"Glorious?" He was laughing in apparent astonishment. "What a curious word to apply to the Imperium. My dear, it's a simple matter of historical necessity. Do you find the law of gravity 'glorious'? My goodness."

"It's very pretty but shouldn't you put it away before someone treads on it?"

"Anla, you raised the topic. I merely wish to prove the elementary facts of life to you before your stubbornness drives me quite mad. Now look at this." He addressed the machine. "Display the number of habitable planets in the universe."

Instantly: $2.51 \ 10^{17}$.

"It's in decimal notation," the gene-sculptor said. "All right, display the current estimated human populations on those planets."

The numbers twinkled: $1 \ 10^{27}$.

Anla tried to think of a one followed by twenty-seven zeroes, but her concentration was not up to it.

"There you are, my dear. Those are the fundamental and irreducible substrates of our civilization. Ten to the eleven galaxies in a variety of fetching shapes and sizes, chockablock with a round octillion human souls. A seething statistical gas of political pressures and competing macromemes. It's a self-organizing stochastic entity, which is just as well for all of us, and the Imperium is its structure."

Anla clutched at the jutting-out portions of her face to stop it flying off, or at least to retard its acceleration. After an interval, during which she concentrated as hard as she could on the ends of her feet, she was able to say in a muffled voice: "Descriptive mumble."

"I beg your pardon?"

"Hang on a bit." She spread her hands and waved the finger-tips vigorously. "You see, I knew you were still there. That's a piss-weak line of argument and you ought to be ashamed of yourself. It's illicit to slide from description to valuation. Most of Earth's empires were based on unabashed slavery. Ours started that way. I don't imagine you'd endorse that, structure or no structure. You like to see slavery?"

The gene man roared with delight. "Of course I do. How else do you suppose a pre-industrial culture can get its resource-surplus to takeoff point? Not much fun for the slaves, I dare say, but quite essential in the big picture."

I won't feel a thing, she thought. Or perhaps I'll feel ten times as much as usual, and it'll go up over the pain threshold. There seemed to be a circle of passive intellectual spectators gathered around them now, the last of the barely conscious.

She moved over to the couch and leaned heavily against the sculptor. "Empire," she told him, "is always the master-slave relationship of a coercive hegemonial state to the affinity-complexes under its dominion. The only justification for an empire comprising the entire universe is that such a structure permits the exercise of your damned predictions. If we all went our own way, your nice little trained bugs could bite each other's bums from now until doomsday without—"

"They're not bugs, my dear, they're memetic hypercycles. Tailored genes in a specified ecology. Surely you're not denying that imperialism is the highest stage of socialism?"

"Oh, I've no doubt you're a good, flag-waving Leninist. But if you want to trade old saws, I can go you one better. Have you ever read any of the early proleptic poems by Asimov? Pre-diaspora, about two thousand years ago."

"Child, I make it a firm rule never to vid the classics. The only Asimov I've ever heard of is the fellow who directed the compilation of the rather arrogantly titled *Asimov's Encyclopedia Galactica*."

"That's his clone. I can't see why you think it's arrogant, he wrote the bloody thing."

The gene-sculptor jerked violently, and managed to get his hand up her skirt. "What, all five thousand volumes?"

"Easy with those fingernails. Yes, he's a demon for work, poor old bugger. There's nothing much else for him to do, he was eighty-nine when they perfected the immortality process. If you're interested, he has a retrospective called *Opus 6000*."

"I'm not. What was the point?"

"The point was that the original Asimov was the first person to posit the sort of civilization we turned out to get. Most of the details were wrong, of course. He didn't know about the Aorist Closure, so he figured we'd get around in spacecraft— you know, like the starwars the kids play. And his Empire only had about as many people as we've got inhabited planets."

"Those figures would have been pretty close to the mark a thousand years ago—"

"But then your dear little bugs wouldn't have had enough to go on, would they? Where he really screwed up, he thought a whole galaxy could be governed with one office clerk for every ten million people. The mind boggles. A neat little team of two thousand nine-to-fivers for each planet. Chariots, I've forgotten the important bit, and I only did the search on this with the kids last month. Here, how do you turn this thing on?"

"Just talk to it. My dear, fascinating as all this is, I'm sorry I ever opened my mouth. Why don't we just go—"

"Hello, look I'm after a reference to a poem by, mark, Isaac Asimov, that's uh A-Z-I-M-"

A pop-up in the index was activated, and the machine began to bellow at her, "*No, no, no*, you benighted imbecile, it's S! *S!* A-S-I-M—"

§

Just at the point where Theri was starting to entertain genuine qualms, of which she was notified by cramps in the stomach and coolness of the skin, Catsize admitted that there was almost certainly not the faintest chance of their being incinerated.

"It's been abandoned for decades, centuries more likely. There'll be no one there except foddles and a few dull machines."

"What, they don't care if you just whip up and nick some of their foddles?" Ben was scandalized.

"Debased currency, my lad. You don't suppose that they still pick the ruth out of foddle-shit, do you, molecule by molecule?

They *make* it, you foolish fellow. Our recent host would be most offended if he thought you thought his thought, or his practise at any rate, wasn't up to synthesizing the odd tonne of immortality promoter."

Now that the satellite was under them instead of in the sky, Theri saw that it was just the standardized crater-and-rill-scape of any other moon. Or was that dark stuff grass? In a single mind-eroding wrench the skite went across the gravity shear of the sanctuary mascon, and they were gusting aerodynamically down to the surface, with the bubble off and warm fake wind in their faces.

"Well, why do they leave them here, then?"

"Why not? Someone else put the gravity in, it's all been amortized, the search for large-scale production of the fabled longevity secret proved to lie in a direction other than the void-ings of foddles, and bureaucrats don't like to be disturbed."

Catsize cut the field. The skite, its lights romantically if unnecessarily extinguished, thumped down to a halt.

Two hundred meters away a vast red-box tree provided world-shade to the sleeping dollops around its trunk. Kael and Catsize dropped to the grass. Ben stumbled and swore. Reluctantly leaving her filament, Theri followed the pale flash of the knife.

They ran across the grass away from her, bent over as low as possible, like an eidetic reconstruction of Kurd or Unilever. Whatever for, they're not going to be mown down by lasers, might as well run completely upright.

One old shag raising her head: the predatory horde freezing, kids playing statues. Three grown men with nothing better to do. The motherly shag, suspicious, coughing consumptively (the name of the ancient disease popping up from a hygiene inlay); fuzzy heads rising; knees creaking; the flock lumbering to its feet.

"Bloody hell!"

Foddles crepitated off in twos and threes, fat littles and old shags scattering to the limits of dim sight. The animals reformed at a safe distance, showing baleful pink eyes.

Funny, Theri mused remotely, planetary populations were exterminated for possession of the mystery in the foddle gastro-intestinal tract. Now the animals dozed in the weak light of a tourist world. Or these ones did. Or had.

Ben sloped off to the north, if that was what it was, knife clutched purposefully. Kael and Theri waited beside the skite. At a signal from Catsize, all four moved to drive the beasts toward the gravity shear interface.

The flock ambled to the invisible barrier and turned smartly left. Theri walked steadily on and glanced at Kael. Is he really so keen, she asked herself, to catch one? He'll let it go after a face-saving struggle.

A foddle broke from the shifting mass and started to canter, followed by two or three others. Kael threw himself at the hind-most shag, struck Theri as she sprang from her side, lost his grip, caught a leg and lay on the moon's surface clutching a kicking foot. Theri took hold of the animal's forelimbs and subdued it. Ten meters off, Catsize lay locked with a fat little.

"Drop that stringy bundle of mange and lend a hand."

They released the frightened beast. By now Catsize was securely astride his little. Ben strolled up with the knife. In silence, all of them regarded the wide gray blade: its margin of sharpness, thinned at the point. A machine ideal in its consonance of form and function, though it was difficult to imagine what the gene sculptor used it for. Hacking up his vegetable protein, presumably. Ben handed the knife to Kael. Quickly, Kael put the blade to the little's throat.

"Not that way," Catsize told him. "Drive the point in behind the windpipe and cut outwards. Two swift moves, the work of a moment."

Kael corrected his stance. Catsize held the foddle's head firmly with both hands and tightened the pressure of his knees on its ribcage.

The moment of truth prolonged itself.

The foddle gave a pitiful bleat. Theri looked at the ground. In a few years, she told herself, the beast would die of its own accord. The longevity drug, ruth, latent in its body, afforded it no immortality. That was the staggering irony. She didn't know if it made slaughtering the foddle more justifiable, or less.

Without her particularly wanting it to, the relevant memory inlay disgorged an outline of the chemical process used to transmute foddle dung into life everlasting. It was closer to a benign infestation than a drug. For the host, the molecular outcome was a homeodynamic somatic equilibrium. Nothing changed except memory and aspiration. Destructive free radicals were obliterated before they could accumulate in cells and do their lethal work. Theri thought briefly of her revolutionary libertarian associates, and their relationship to the Imperial authorities, and smiled with a kind of suppressed fright at the analogy. She looked across to the trapped foddle, sensed the bodies of her friends caught in the immobility of terminal choice, breath held in their lungs, ready for release with the releasing of the creature's blood.

"Okay, Catsize. If you know so much about it, you do it."

Kael retired to stand beside Theri, putting his arm along her shoulder, but she stood closed again within herself and regarded the ground.

"Damn it, I'm the pilot, not the bloody cook. Here." The thing was proffered handle-first to Theri.

Visions of lusty, contemptuous Anla. She'd take the knife and with clean efficient strokes cut the miserable creature's neck, hand the limp, bloody carcass to her husband, walk off.

"Not me, let it go."

Theri shifted her feet and looked at the sky. An edge of burning light on the world Newstralia. Clouds streaked the curve of its blue. She saw an elephant in one cloud-mass; in a minute it would be mounting the north pole.

The situation had become altogether ridiculous; the buzz of the party was wearing off.

"Well, let's take it back to our little holiday home and work out how we'll do it in the morning." Compromise was Kael's specialty.

They straggled back to the skite, the foddle draped over Kael's shoulders, all of them bearing their reprieved pride.

§

Beached and abandoned on the margins of sleep, Anla found once again that though many of her friends swore by this state of consciousness it had taken on for her the aspect of an anti-*tsunami*. Sleep's enormous combers withdrew to the horizon without a glance over their shoulders. In the quarter gravity of the unlit sleeping chamber, excellent as it was for gymnastic screwing, or as presumably it would be given a competent partner, she was queasy and bored.

Issues of metaphysical sturdiness came to her attention, as they'd been known to do, provisionally penned in the kennels to which she'd assigned them, whimpering for the final disposition she was fairly unlikely to make on their behalf.

Morality was one. She was certainly no stranger to the problems of axiology.

Lovely word, that. Axiology: *theory of value*. It seemed to contain its own solutions: axe your way through the Gordian knot, acts of piety, access to truth.

Ralf was proving to be a snorer; she kicked him peevishly, and he rolled lightly on the webbing without waking.

Why should Ralf's profession seem to her so self-evidently odious, while he happily accepted it as the epitome of a right-thinking life? Calling him a dull shit, and adducing his ineptitude at fornication as *ad hominem* evidence, was hardly exhaustive, not to a midnight philosopher. Ah no, she'd been this way before. It kept coming back to that silly question: "Why should we be moral?"

A surprisingly large number of people thought that you should be, and even considered it to be a moral obligation. Ha ha, boom boom. But suppose you used the word "should" as an evaluative and motivational expression, instead of a normative one? If you wish to climb to the top of the mountain, you should walk up rather than down, or stumble round in circles.

Of course last time she'd come along this track she'd detected a snag with "evaluative", too, but that was on the next level up and you had to start somewhere.

All right, take Ralfo as your representative simple unreflecting man. Persuade him of the vileness of imperialism. Crisis for Ralf. Echoing voids of doubt, disillusion and guilt. Never again, as the poet said, will he be certain that what he imagines are the clear dictates of moral reason are not merely the ingrained and customary beliefs of his time and place. Anla allowed herself a fanfare of trumpets, bowing graciously.

Okay, so then he might ask himself what he could do in the future to avoid prejudices and provincial mores, or, more to the point, almost universally accepted mores—and thus to discover what he *really* ought to do.

That was merely another normative enquiry, though; the tough one was "show me that there is some form of behavior which I am *obliged* to endorse."

Moral constraint seemed to mean either that you should pursue good ends and eschew bad ones, or that you should be faithful to one or more correct rules of conduct. Greeks and Taoists versus Hebrews and Confucians, yeah, yeah.

Chariots, it was incredible to think that they'd been chewing on this for upward of four thousand years without coming to a definitive, intuitively overwhelming conclusion. But then the imperial ideologists thought they had, didn't they, with their jolly old stochastic memetic-extrapolatory hedonic calculus or whatever the fuck they were calling it these days. The least retardation of optimal development for the greatest number, world without end, or at least until the trend functions blur out. So they managed to get both streams of thought into one ethical scholium without solving *anything*. After all, why obey a rule like that? And who gets to define as "good" those magical parameters making up the package called "optimal development"?

The besieged libertarians on Chomsky, she thought darkly,

might differ from Ralf on the question of the good life.

Anyway, even if we all agreed that certain parameters were good, why should that oblige us to promote their furtherance? It might be prudent good sense to do so, and aesthetically pleasing, and satisfy some itch we all have, and save us from being raped in the common, but then the sublime constraining force you sort of imagine the idea of moral obligation having just evaporates into self-serving circumspection.

Admittedly there was that tricky number of Kant's about us possessing a rational nature, and being *noumena* instead of brute *phenomena*, and thus not being able to act immorally without self-contradiction, but any fool could see that that went too far on the one hand and not far enough on the other, and anyway what was wrong with a bit of self-contradiction if you stopped when you needed eye implants?

Anla giggled to herself, and wondered where Ben and the others had got to. He was probably off by himself gloomily hastening the day of the ophthalmologist. Well, was leaving Ben to his own devices a matter for moral self-rebuke?

Shit, you'd think this bastard could do something to the genes in his nasal cavity.

This man can see into the future. Fucking incredible, really, you just rip out a few million eigenvectors from your mathematical sketch of an octillion human beings, what's that in hydrogen molecules, say three and a bit by ten to the twenty-three to the gram, into ten to the twenty-seven, shit, brothers and sisters, we're statistically equal to three kilograms of hydrogen gas, yes, you plump for the major characteristics you think you'd like to play with and code them up into genes and build yourself a little memetic beastie that stands in for what you figure pushes and pulls thee and me and all our star-spangled relatives, and you breed the little buggers in a tasty itemized soup and watch the way the mutants go.

Wonderful, Ralf. Bug-culture precapitulates bugged-culture. No way we can jump you won't know about in advance, because the little bugs snitched on us.

Have you ever wondered, Ralf, if we're all just a big stochastic biotic projection for the Charioteers? See how we run.

But you don't let us mutate, do you, Ralf? That's where you fumbled the ball, Dr A, in your ancient poems. The Empire will never fall. We will live forever, and the boring Empire with us.

Anla lashed out viciously with her foot.

"Will you fucking stop *snoring*!"

§

The skite shot across Ralf's deserted dropspace, lights splashing the deserted studio. The party was well and truly over. One vehicle remained, snug under weather-shield. The sculptormobile presumably.

"She must've got a lift back, Ben."

The shared lie would last them back to the alien, familiar city, would keep the certainty of Anla, lying low in the arms of the enemy somewhere in the dark dacha, at one remove from reality for another hour.

Ben took the knife in his right hand, while his left continued to stroke the foddle's reprieved neck. For a second the blade stood against the light-spattered sky (was it the same galaxy as home? he couldn't remember), its point between his thumb and index finger. It spun twice, then, thudded into the timber door, and stuck there, quivering, above the star-like brass knob.

3.

Brisk G2 sunlight, slanting to the bed, woke Theri.

Small bubbles had long since formed and burst in the duro-bond ceiling, and little shards hung like leaves ready to fall. A glo-panel, its adhesion waning like the gravitational constant, had broken away at one end from its induction surface.

A fly circled through the sunlight, wings glinting, and shot suddenly to the panel. It hung upside down for a few seconds, cleaning its legs, before strolling across to peruse the horizon of its flat-earth world.

Theri turned her face away from the sun and kissed Kael's neck. It wasn't often they woke in contact with each other, like this, though they usually drifted to sleep in some sort of embrace. Sighing, she resumed her catalogue of their holiday room.

A collection of holograms smiled from the mantelpiece in random directions: cognates, presumably, or ancestors, of the people who'd rented them the house. From the largest frame an elderly youth in mortarboard and academic gown looked down, a slightly bewildered expression on his mustachioed face. He clutched a roll of paper to his chest.

Strange how you could tell he wasn't a baby. Some hint of desperation in his eyes. Must have worked for years at night for that thing, chasing the education he'd missed in his frontier youth. Earning enough in daytime drudgery to pay for his clan-kin or to meet his world's amortization debt; hurrying to evening peptide shots, scouring his Databank, cudgeling his brains through the law of torts and the case of Imperator vs Boggs.

And now caught by the laser on his final triumphant day, the image providing documentary evidence just as necessary and admissible as the rolled-up diploma in his hand and the numerical record filed forever with maximum precautionary redundancy in deep core.

Maybe they ought to grant degrees carved on blocks of stone, something with a bit of substance to it, something to put you at risk of a hernia every time you picked it up.

Theri sat up in bed, looked down at her lover: graduate educer now, due shortly to join Anla in her profession. If not in her avocation as libertarian revolutionary. He slept on his back with his mouth half open, showing his teeth. Strong, even teeth, one of his best features, giving a bit of firmness to the softness of his mouth. His mouth was weak, really, and small.

The bristles on his face took the alien sunlight like unevenly worn sandpaper, growing thick along his upper lip and chin, patchy along his jaw. Theri occasionally persuaded him to grow a beard, but he always smeared it off after two or three weeks, finding some pretext for being clean cheeked. He might instead have used an enzyme boost, and flowered like a prophet, but that was hardly old Socrates' style.

She slid her fingers into his hair which fanned out, matted and leonine, on the pillow. Fine, light hair; her fingers caught in a knot and pulled at his scalp. Kael shifted a little, turning his head. Not wanting him to wake yet, she drew back.

The hoot of a cargo-vessel, long and muffled, came from the harbor, warning swimmers and free craft of its impending set down. Someone clattered around in the back garden of the terrace. Ben or Catsize, up already.

That Neanderthal scientist, Ben, she reflected, had produced a fine endogenous black beard after he'd married Anla. It lent him the look of a half-crazed frontier doctor. The sort of physician who loomed out of the midnight rain on a broken-down hack, delivered the badly breached baby in the nick of time, cursed the lack of trained midwives and civilized pharmaceuticals, revived the expiring mother with a quick whiff of pungents instead, conjured an ampoule of buzz from the soaked pocket of his frock-coat, shot half, passed the rest to the tribe, and disappeared into the rain again.

The mad doctor probably hadn't slept at all. Theri slipped from the bed and padded to the window. There was Ben, working his way along the garden fence, checking for chinks, securing the gate (no classy safe-fields at these rental prices), creating a haven for last night's foddle.

She could see the animal eagerly chewing the rented grass, its little teeth crunching rhythmically, its head nodding purposefully. Industrious little beast, building useless ruth precursors with every chomp.

Christ, she thought, they can't really be going to kill that thing, for all the forbidden delights of its nonsynthesized proteins. We'd look pretty stupid waiting around for Anla to come home and slay it for us.

Pity about Anla and Ben, but that's their style, here or on Victoria or anywhere. Anla taking off with some impossible man. Ben wandering around gloomily picking his nose, going for walks, competing without heart with a chessmaster program. Two days, three, never longer. Anla returning: triumphant, unrepentant, radiant.

Lusty wench, our Anla, long black hair and long fingers, good at haranguing the masses and telling everyone where they get off and what's what.

Anla floating around the house as if nothing has happened. Ben almost catatonic with sullenness, vidding his library. Bright Anla coming and going through the rooms of the house with no interface to his gloomy world.

Suddenly the recriminations, the real hurt out in the open. Anla flaring back. A day, a day and a half, of hot angry words. Reconciliation. All's well for another couple of months. Been going on for four orthoyears now, Theri thought, funny way to live. Not like me and the sleeping Socrates, but at least each of *them* knows what the other thinks.

What have *you* been thinking about, Kael, as we've drifted through this holiday? Eating and drinking our way around Newstralia. Relaxed and expansive in the cafes and restaurants, feeding your face with garlic crustaceans cooked in oil, with crisp-skinned nightingsnail, with felafel, with ednafish in puce-bean sauce. And in the long afternoons in the buzz gardens of half-deserted pubs and in the garden of this house and this strange bedroom?

Kael, what goes on behind your blue eyes, your warm sleepy words? Are you happy with me on those littered beaches, among the bodies and the crushed cups, or in the crowds under the garish lights, making fun of the vulgar feelie come-ons with their neuroinducers limited by law to a zone no greater than three-quarters of the width of the sidewalk so that prudes of both sexes blanch at the tingle in their loins; what do you think of me at times like that?

A good man at keeping your own counsel, not one for the claws of argument, the knives of passion.

Kael, sweet Kael, what goes on in your head? What do I know about you, or you about me? All we've really done here is put on mass in the wrong places and celebrate a mutual languid happiness, an absence of tension. We've got nothing to be tense about. I really mustn't eat so much, neither of us must.

§

In silence, barely awake, Kael watched through half closed eyes his Theri spread her elbows like wings.

Standing by the window, she ran her hands over her stomach, straightened her back and tightened the muscles of her abdomen. Her hair flowed down her back almost to her bum—a nice bum, white from the kini.

Kael felt, even if he did not see, her splayed fingers pressing from her pelvic arch, across her belly, up over the jut of her ribcage, passing to right and left of her breasts. Theri stretched, crucified on the morning (nice image, that, he thought; at least the Christers' fifth millennial comeback has done some small good, even if it's turned Theri into a masochist), and she pivoted with the sunlight on her face and shoulders, and padded barefoot to the door. Funny toes the girl's got.

She reached for her sombrero, breasts silhouetted. Sweet tits for the holding. Theri under the black sombrero drew an imaginary weapon, took steady aim at the helpless Kael.

The invisible flash would have blinded him if he hadn't had his eyes nearly closed.

Theri spun the gun nonchalantly on her index finger, slid it easily into a holster low on her hip, and left, sombrero aslant, for the shower.

Kael lay back and looked at the autumnal ceiling in the summer's light. Resurrected, he too was now well-armed. Get her when she comes back from the shower, her skin moist, teach her some real shooting.

Bang!

"Charioteers!"

Kael leapt from his bed, hot-footed it to the amenities. Theri stood affrighted against the farther wall, sombrero resting upside down in the open stillcell. The faintest mist of warm moisture drifted to the charged lining of the cell. Efficient Kael glanced at the readout panel, adjusted the field, reset the fail-safes. He turned and stared at her.

"It's almost impossible, what you just did," he said mildly.

She stamped her foot. There were goosebumps on her skin. "Don't start."

"It's not hard to understand how to operate it, little, really it isn't. You must put a terrific lot of effort into not understanding, actually. Still, what I don't understand is how you managed what you just did."

"I mean it, don't start. Piss off and let me wash myself in peace."

"It's quite an old invention, petal, though not as old as, say, the wheel. They designed it to conserve water, my dear Theri, because a lot of Newstralia is a dune planet. See, there's this pulsed spherical forcefield that gulps in a lot of air and squeezes it very hard to wring the water out of it, which also heats the aforementioned liquid to the desired temperature. What you did, my bundle, was make the field expand instead of contract before it switched off, and all the air rushed very fast into the vacuum and made a big noise."

"I can't hear you, shithead," she said from within the still-cell. "Anyway, that sounds like a lot of garbage to me. What happens when the field is contracting and a new lot of air is coming in, eh? answer me that. Why doesn't that create a vacuum, smart-arse? And what makes you assume it was my fault, there are five people in this house, all I did was turn it on, after all, so the statistical likelihood that I caused it to happen is one in five, hardly overwhelming odds as I think even you will be obliged to agree."

"Ah, but you were the proximate agent, and this is not the

first such occasion. Indeed, if we multiply the number of times such baffling technological failures have taken place in your immediate vicinity, I imagine we'd come closer to figures of, oh, say one in several millions, without straining our memories. And if you can't follow the simple train of thought involved in my lucid description of the principle involved, there's no doubt in my mind that an unprejudiced jury of your peers would take this as *prima facie*— Umph. What are you— Stop that at once, my girl, what would your parents—"

§

Theri and Kael at screw in the still-cell. A warm rain, the hidden pulsing field doing its job discreetly and well. Gentle Kael meek and mild holding back his loved one's face. Purple horseshoes on Kael's shoulders. I meant it to hurt, it's not enough. Theri coming gently, with frustrated tenderness, in the exploding shower of a rented terrace on an alien world.

§

They strolled later down El Cheapo Street, favorite address of babies here on vacation, the spine of a fairly fetid slum still clinging to a distinctive identity from the most primitive years of the planet's initial colonization.

It was a jumble of old stone and rusting iron, wrought and heaved into place by human and animal muscle-power. Warped lanes twisted to the waterfront, open balconies transformed into enclosed living space by sheets of buckling durobond.

A flamboyant ornithopter, vividly striped in applegreen and red, flapped low overhead, making for the more opulent surf beaches away from the harbor. Kael held Theri's hand loosely.

Catsize and Ben emerged from a free-enterprise commissary, Ben carrying a box of food, foils and loaves and a stick of salami visible at the top. Catsize labored under a rather large crate of lettuce or some vegetable resembling it.

"What the hell do you take us for, a colony of rabbits?"

"Not at all, my good man, these are William's rations."

"Who?"

"William Wool, our fuzzy little foddle friend from last night's woeful expedition, now at play in our garden."

"But he's meant to provide *us* with food. And what's wrong with grass, anyway?"

"Not enough, and of an inferior quality."

"Some foddle rustler you are."

"No less than certain others. Good day to you both."

§

The handouts of lettuce were devoured in seconds. Ben opened the door and summoned William Wool. The beast dashed at once across the newly desolate garden. Never entirely convincing as a garden, now it was a doleful sight: grass chewed to the quick, shrubs mere tattered remnants, bark frayed to kindling.

The foddle hurtled past Ben's legs and stood in the kitchen babbling for milk. He removed its ribbon and tinkling bell— pilfered on its behalf by Catsize from the untenanted cage of some domestic or decorative bird—and outfitted William Wool to face the world. A heavy leather collar ferocious with studs replaced the ribbon, a length of almost invisible monomer providing the requisite contact between man and client.

Ben and William trailed up El Cheapo: a kick for the worrying dog, a hard stare for the clucking shopper. Human and foddle turned into the park.

Placing his back against an alien piece of flora, and his buttocks in contact with dirt and grass, Ben paid out the line. Ecstatically, William lifted his tail and poured forth a little steam of the celebrated stuff of legend. Ben wished a large amount of it on his faithless wife's head. Whore.

From across the park an official was approaching officiously, park-keeper's tricorn on his waxed hair, spiked stick of office in his hand, imperial guardian of public decorum.

Oh Anla, you bitch, what would I be if I'd never met you? She had made him what he was, she and that lunatic Catsize; Anla, with her ideas and visions, Catsize with his thousand personae and half-crazed fantasies.

Ben roused himself from melancholy to the task at hand. It had to be admitted that the uses of mindfuck was one of Catsize's more valuable contributions to his entity.

"You can't have animals in this park."

"It only says dogs."

"Most people don't have, what is it, foddles."

"That's just the point, isn't it?"

"What?"

"This is a foddle sanctuary. It says 'No Dogs' to protect the innocent littles and their defenseless shags."

"You trying to be funny, mate?"

"It's hardly a laughing matter."

"Bloody right." The park-keeper spied the small steaming pile and stared at it in outrage. "Anyhow, what are you doing with a foddle? They're a protected fauna."

This was more tricky; it was a point which had not occurred to Ben. "Precisely my point."

"Well, where did you get it?"

Ben allowed his arm to rise slowly until his hand, with one finger extended, had subtended a full quadrant of the sky.

"This foddle is normally resident in the special sanctuary allocated to its kind on the nearby moon, which you see up there. Oh, it must have gone down. Now, in order for the creatures to maintain their health and keep in good general overall nick, they are obliged to return at intervals to the bracing rigors of a gravitational field approximately equal in strength to the one in which their species evolved. It's a sort of holiday for them."

"That's as may be, mate, but *what's this one doing in my park?*"

Ben regarded the strangled outburst with astonishment. "But this is a travelling stock reserve."

"Don't try to put one over on me, mate, this is a municipal park and I've been working for the council for eighty-seven years this July."

"Then I take it you'll be acquainted with the Lands Appropriation and Uses Act of 2853 (amended 3102)?"

"Eh?" The man drew back a step, suddenly wary.

"The provisions of the Act make it mandatory and binding on all councils to provide a stopping place for livestock of not less than two hectares and such stock as are watered there are to be adequately protected at the council's expense. You can look it up if you don't believe me."

"What are ya, a high court judge or something?"

"I have a working knowledge of the law and I cannot too strongly advise you not to molest my animal. This planet was built on foddle dung, you know."

The keeper muttered off, a temporary respite at least.

Ben's good humor collapsed. Rotten, rotten whore.

§

The ferry slid on its modest laminar lift-field over the darkening water, the vast squat tower of the Teleport Authority swinging astern behind the rail's scrollwork, blotting out a distant section of twinkling affluence in Rose Red, the margins of dormitory bureaucracy.

After the long day's humid swelter, the harbor was finally cooling. Waves slipped dark and oily under the ferry's bows. The clang and rush of an autonomic cleaner emptying its foaming tank from the stern of a loading surface freighter came sullenly through the soupy air.

Theri leaned her head against Kael's neck and smelt the sand and salt in his hair, her shoulders burning slightly under the weight of his arm.

Turning, hoisting herself up on the rail, she let her head fall back until she was peering into the gray whistling vault of the sky. It was thick with skites, neatly tracking their beams, lofty empyrean godlings with no part or interest in the nautical sphere which she and Kael skimmed.

"Do you suppose Anla will be back yet?"

"Tomorrow's more likely."

"What are we going to do with the foddle?"

"Take it back to the moon, I suppose."

If we can't even murder a foddle, Theri thought, what chance do we have against an Empire? But surely that was to look at the matter from the wrong end. Or was it? It was easy enough to predict sweet-and-gentle Kael's view of the matter, but she would rather hear Anla's.

The ferry docked tidily above the softly slapping wavelets at the foot of El Cheapo Street. They jumped ashore before the gap between vessel and wharf had quite closed. The utterly minimal potential for self-destruction in this act did not prevent phobic groans and tuts from several of their presumably much older fellow passengers.

As the ferry pulled away once more, three leatherlace vested goons at the distant top of the hill activated anti-friction shields and hurled themselves head first and belly down in its direction, providing more ghastly thrills for the cautious centenarians on board.

One of these louts slammed past centimeters from Kael's leg, hooting the while. There was some satisfaction in seeing him overshoot at the wharf, zip briefly across the filthy water, and sink like a stone.

White petals of some nameless fragrant tree hung over the rented terrace's fence. A skite of similar hue crunched down angrily opposite the tree.

"The sculptormobile?"

"Probably. Uh-huh."

Anla tripped lightly across the pavement and entered the house ahead of them. The skite rose jerkily, going whence it had come.

At the foot of the hill, the body-skier's helplessly guffawing companions were guiding out a buoy.

§

Anla, Ben and Catsize formed an engaging tableau in the kitchen. Ben glanced up from his diligent library-vidding to note the arrival of Kael and Theri, grunted a form of greeting, returned to his studies. This was clearly a more expansive welcome than his wife had been privileged to receive.

Anla threw herself into a chair with resigned aplomb. "Hello, you two."

"Hello, Anla petal, come back to us have you?" Kael, trying his hand at banter. "Thought you'd run away, did you? Our little holiday home wasn't good enough for you, is that it? And after all we've done for you, Working and slaving to give you some of the things we could never afford ourselves. That's your way of showing gratitude, is it? But you come back smart enough when you want a good feed, don't you?"

Anla smiled blandly, while Ben concentrated on his library display with the intensity of a recluse; the atmosphere clung denser than ever. Blithely unaffected by her spouse's rejection, the unease of her friends, Anla continued her placid chair-sitting.

Catsize filled a vessel with milk, placed it squarely in the center of the kitchen floor, opened the back door. The foddle uttered a glad ejaculation and fell on the liquid, lapping like a dog.

"What the hell's that?'

"Allow me to introduce Mr. William Wool, our dinner."

"Charioteers, you go away for a day and they turn the place into a zoo."

Catsize caught Theri's eye, gave Kael the nod. The three enskited, off for a buzz or two in a public house, to find a party, to stay clear of the house for some time.

§

Anla put her feet on the table and considered her Ben. Were

she to go to bed first he would sleep in his chair, but if he preceded her it would be beneath his dignity to allow anything so insignificant as his spouse to cause him to move.

She watched his somber bearded face as he bent over the tiny dancing sigils. He seemed set for the night. She listened to the steady hum of the old clock. The tired hoot of some night-embarking craft rose from the harbor.

Anla stood up and silently made a pot of tea, placing a mug at Ben's elbow, and returned to her chair. Ben let the tea cool, abandoned the library at length and walked to the cold-field. He poured himself a tot of chilled milk, picked up a hardcopy of some Sinese poems Catsize had left lying around, sat down at the kitchen bench.

Anla started to doze. She tried to keep herself awake by thinking of the gene-sculptor. A fool really, kept patting his hair into place, even while he was trying to keep his end up. Macromemes, indeed.

Ben rose slowly from his chair and climbed the stairs to bed. Ralf had a lift-shaft, of course: one floated in it like a leaf. Anla looked at the clock: 0320, about bloody time too, give him half an hour. She was wretchedly tired.

When she slipped into bed, Ben was so fast asleep that he didn't move his legs to make room for her. The planet pulled unremittingly at her bones. Now that she'd become accustomed to Ralf's quarter gravity bed, she craved its costly comfort.

§

Catsize galloped up the stairs in the hot morning and gave the door a healthy kick.

"You two want any breakfast?"

"I do, but not this bloody whore."

"Don't call me whore, you bastard. I'll come down for mine, Catsize."

The poet bowed low to the dumb worm-chewed door. "As Madame and Monsieur wish."

He tripped lightly to the kitchen and gave Kael and Theri the thumbs-up. "Contact between our friends has, I judge, been established."

4.

On the last evening of their holiday, Anla sent them all out of the house, Ben included. When they returned with prime buzz, melancholy and self-satisfied in the floral sunset air, the kitchen sang with mouth-watering deliciousness.

Anla sat them down, and fetched soft lights, and brought out to the table a steaming rack of foddle, all brown without and pink within and spiced with herbs. It was the finest food they'd ever eaten.

§

Well pleased by the macabre feast, Catsize took a constitutional stroll in the Newstralian darkness. Licking one finger, he meditated on the semiotics of the event, on its vile, unthinking, utterly representative sexism, and on the curious species of rebuttal, implicit in it, of just that prejudice.

How monstrously hard, he thought, how unfair, to have to tote two millennia of baggage in your head. Yet all good and bad was, in any case, decaying, degrading, disintegrating; every small gain was a mockery of things ineluctably lost.

The poet squinted at the botched constellations, fancying that he might pick out Chomsky's star. But the anarchists were skittish tonight. Yes, locked behind their defenses. He had little hope for them; as little, perhaps, as they held for him.

§

In the night, Ben and Anla sat on the dock steps watching the faint glow of energized yacht sails. The tide brought a procession of emblems: a log, a torn foil, a dead fish. The belly of the fish took the foddle moon's light like a skull. Ben kissed his wife gently, running his tongue over hers. She held him at bay for a lingering moment before responding electrically, forcing his head back, thrusting her hand into his kilt. Ben broke free, probing at his lip. Blood.

She looked unblinking at his face. "Standing up against the wall."

"Yes," he said. They tore at one another.

PART TWO

1.

There was no frontier roughing-it about the Imperial Teleport Authority's facilities on Newstralia, you had to give them that. From the moment he and Catsize and Kael had seen the others of their party off at the Women's Departure Lounge, they'd been processed with the deft efficiency of bytes in a sublime computer. Nevertheless, the officially ordained segregation from his wife caused Ben to chew at his lip.

So far as he knew there had never been a failure on the part of the ancient Aorist Discontinuity to deliver body and soul safely from star to star. Well, provided, of course, that you sensibly adhered to the vector limitations specified in your rating. Briefly, a horrid image of arriving at the far end of the universe, gaunt and asphyxiated and dead, caused Ben's guts to contract.

That was stupid, in turn, because you'd run out of breath long before you perished of starvation. But it was precisely such superstitious anxieties that made separation from your women, sorry Anla, woman, so difficult to bear. It couldn't be helped that you had to go through the Aorist gate alone, but it was inhuman that you were prevented on inane and arbitrary grounds from holding your loved one's hand (unless you were gay, and even then it was frowned on as tasteless) right up to the last moment.

But you have to go through...*nude!* he jeered at himself in a Clan mother's voice. After all, men and women can't be allowed to mingle freely where they might glimpse each other's...parts.

He considered Catsize's small, droll, bare-arsed figure moving ten meters ahead of him on the slipfield, undergoing the inexorable scrutiny and pre-transit operations with the panache of a seasoned voyager. Ben attempted the same complacency while the clever machines plumbed his genotype, re-rated him, injected him with the memory proteins constituting the address co-ordinates of Victoria in relation to Newstralia, totted up the fiscal credit in his Creditbank account and coded that as well, inlaying the balance after service fees to a region of his hypothalamus tied to his respiration reflexes and tagged with the autonomic "tamper-and-abort" sequence.

Not a human face to be seen during the process; too slow, too vulnerable, too...human.

Again, one could hardly complain. With several billion transits through any given planet's gates each orthoyear, and only, what was it, 128 Charioteer discontinuity centers on the planet, some of them lost long ago to plate movements, and 1024 gates in each of them.... Ben's fingers plucked uselessly for his library, but he'd surrendered that hired instrument minutes earlier.

Anyway, it was no wonder they bunged you through at the rate of one every two minutes. What must it be like at one of the Imperial Bureaux worlds? What must it be like on bloody old Earth?

A machine spoke to him firmly, and he gave it his clothes. The air, naturally, was pleasantly warm and its humidity and ionization were judged to a nicety.

He slipped out of the realm of instruments into the spiral holding pattern, his sanitized seat moving forward through a huge crowd of naked, circling men toward the entrance to anywhere.

"Excuse me, may I walk with you a little?"

Ben looked up in alarm. "Get back to your seat, dickhead, you'll screw up the whole entry sequence. You've probably already lost your place—they'll send you back to the start and charge you an indemnity."

"Oh no, I'm not a voyager." Above his earnest eyes, anchored in the supra-orbital bulge, twin rosy tendrils waved. His hairless skin was pale green, and furrowed at the brow. A spot of cosmetic genetics, and less grotesque than some Ben had seen. "Tell me," the pseudo-alien said solicitously, "do you have an interest in the spiritual life?"

There were several ways of coping with this. "What are you, a sex fiend? just because I've got no trousers on doesn't— I'm not budging my backside off this seat for anything, see?"

Green skin blushes to a kind of dirty brown, an engaging effect. "Bless me, brother, I assure you I have only spiritual matters to discuss. Since you are about to undergo the Sacramental Translocation—"

It had been a lame opening. Ben changed his tack, watching the hundreds of heads and shoulders ahead of him glide closer to the place where space held hands with itself. "Yeah, sorry cobber, can't be too careful. But now I see by your outfit that you are a Chao boy."

"Certainly not!" Indignantly, the green man drew several items from a bag. "You mistake me for a communicant of the dissident Illuminatus faction. My faith is the faith of the Ubiquitous Christ, shortly to return with his angels the Charioteers and bear witness to the good tidings."

Ben rubbed dubiously at his chin, pondering these facts. "Well.... Can't say that I agree, can't say I don't neither. Wasn't He supposed to come again in the year 4000?"

"No, no, a common misconception," the missionary said, without altering his lugubrious expression. "The date set down—and you'll find that this is confirmed by leading scientists—is 4004 AD, at eight p.m. on October 22. Mere months away! Will you be with him, brother?"

Ah Catsize, he should have chosen you. "Sir, you come close to persuading me. On the other hand—" Ben pulled judiciously at his lower lip.

"Glory be, brother, the evidence is abundant." The advocate of Christ Charioteer propped an unfolded holo against his chest and expounded glumly. "The teachings of our founder, the Sainted Irving Macher, in his scriptures *Blinkie Heaven*—"

"What faith is that again?"

"The Church of the Lost Tribes of Enoch in Britain, Earth," the apostle declared with rapturous gloom. "As you can see, by utilizing the ancient wisdom of Gematria and Logomancy, the great Truths become instantly apparent." In racy cerise script, the word CHARIOTEERS sparkled on his display. "Let me ask you this one question, brother. Is it a mere accident that the ancient and vanished race which built the Teleport network linked into it only those planets in this wide starry universe which are sufficiently like our home world to support human life unaided? Is it no more than a cosmic fluke that J. Peter White the great anthropologist stumbled on the first known Aorist Discontinuity while studying little known mysteries of the past? At the very moment in Humankind's troubled history that population pressures were driving our species to the edge of extinction? Can you imagine, with your feeble mind—"

"Here, steady on."

"But our minds *are* feeble, brother, by comparison with that glorious lost race which constructed and gave into our care the keys to universal kingdom. Unlimited horizons! Did you know that that's what 'aorist' means? 'Unlimited'?" the man asked in less fervent tones.

"Well, yes, but it also means 'indefinite' which could suggest that Jesus hasn't quite made up his mind about when—"

"Set your fears at rest! For behold: when AORIST is removed," and those six letters flared to violet, and vanished, "the sacred name of those constructors becomes CHEER. The good tidings written in the skies at His birth! You know, be of good CHEER?'

"Yeah, pretty convincing all right. But look, mate, I'll be going through in a tick."

"Shortly, then, you shall be blessed with contact with the ineffable. Observe: without the RITE of ER," blue flames dropping from the refurbished slogan, "the mighty plans of the CHARIOTEERS are lost in CHAOS," and the remaining letters, black ash smoking faintly, closed up to prove that it was so.

The stream of chairs on the laminar flux had straightened now, and plunged toward the Aorist Discontinuity gate, ancient mystery enough for any man, each seat plucked magnetically from the path at the last moment and drawn, empty, to begin again its endless loop.

"ER? What's the Rite of ER?"

"Elizabeth Regina, brother, the monarch of the Britannic Isles at the time of the discovery of the Teleport miracle. A clear sign from Enoch to the Lost Tribes."

Ben settled himself back in his seat, his belly closing in on itself again, fear rising. Anla, have you gone through yet? Or have you changed your mind and nicked back for another quickie with your latest lover, you crazy tart? "But you haven't said where Jesus comes into it, mate. I reckon that'd be pretty crucial."

"Can't you see?" the green man cried in triumph, authentic emotion activating his features. The letters shuffled one final time, and the name CHRIST blazed in gold. The discarded phonemes faded swiftly from sight, but not before Ben could pounce with equal and opposite triumph.

"AOEER?" he said incredulously. "REEOA? EAR EO?"

"A theological mystery too subtle for discussion at this point," explained the cleric, and yelped as automatic safety devices snatched him off the ground and carted him away. His display burst into massed sacred song as he ascended. Unabashed, he lobbed a small faxed volume into Ben's unprotected lap. "Bear the Master's words with you into the Place of Mystery and pray that your eyes might be opened."

The seat slid to a halt before the eye-haunting void of the Aorist Discontinuity, and invisible forces lifted Ben and thrust him unhesitatingly into the nothingness where Act and Potency are one.

Like grass blown in a warm wind, his brain was interrogated by the archaic, incomprehensible artifact; inlayed memory molecules responded with ZIP code and particulars; the field took hold of him and hurled him on his way even as he yelled back, "The bloody thing won't be transmitted, you cretinous bast—"

Thoughts cold and hazy. No-time began.

2.

On an elastic strand of associations, Ben's sharp, frosty perceptions twanged to an hallucinatory recall of his virgin launch, four orthoyears earlier, through the Aoristic Closure.

Oh I know him well, this baby scientist of nineteen, stranded on a tropical continent in the long rows of grape vines that marched endlessly across the red dirt. Ben on the upward mobility kick, earning with the sweat of his brow a bit of exchange value in the long vacation, fulfilling his numerous parents' fantasies.

It was all coming, then: initial degree in a thousand days or so; a good job in a data-farm, with prospects of rising in the ranks of the Imperial bureaucracy; cognatic espousal to little Jini and the others, pimples and ponytails; a nice apartment in the clan-house with a tending machine so that Jini wouldn't have to mother the baby by hand like the mums had to do with me and Julia (but the stupid bastards, that was supposed to be the whole wonderful point of it all). And the tiny grandchildren, rushing upstairs to see the nanas and grampas, providing endless anecdotes for the neighbors' delectation, soaking up little bonnets and booties and rompers as fast as they could clack from the knitting needles.

It was all they had ever wanted, it was all Jin and Soo and Flo and the others had ever wanted, it was probably all I wanted then. Sunspots that year had raddled the phones, so Jin sent a text letter to my library, seven thousand kilometers to the vineyards:

dearest ben, just a short note to say how much we miss you. bolte is real dull when your not here. i went out with Jak and Soo to the feelies. just the three of us, i felt real lonely without you, what with Jak cuddling Soo in the dark and me just thinking of you all those leagues away picking grapes, though Jak did give me a cuddle on the way home. Soo has bought a new sari from the free commissary. she looks stunning in it. i'm going to get a shorty with my next pay but i won't wear it till you come back.

And so it went on, I read every word of it, and started to clear it from Holding but put it into Longterm Store instead, choky with some species of sentiment, stood in the dust and tore at the vines thinking of the night I'd left on the ballistic freighter.

You'd panted in my ear then, little tubby Jini, and I managed to get my hand between your camisole and bodice—one layer nearer than usual.

That was some triumph, Jin, squirming around on the seats of that steamed-up skite. "Oh Ben I love you, don't please, Ben, don't, someone's coming, it's Jak and Soo."

And it was Jak and Soo, coming back from their roll around on the beach. Not that Soo was much value in that department either, and Flo's virtue was a byword.

Ben and Jak and Soo and Jin was the regular team, fiancés and fiancées chaperoning one another in a spare clapped-out Clan Griffith skite. There was a four week cycle. Every second week it would be his turn to spend half an hour on the beach or in the park while Jak and Jin and Jak and Soo enjoyed the superior amenities of the skite.

Alternately, Jak would vacate the plastic upholstery in favor of Ben and Soo or Ben and Jin. Chariots, what a thickwit, coming back to the skite giggling and nudging,

"Now, now, you two, I hope you haven't been up to anything we wouldn't do."

And bugger me, we hadn't had we? Not anything you wouldn't

do with the girls, Jak, because you were going to marry them like I was, weren't you, and the agreement was that we wouldn't spoil the merchandise. Not that there was any chance of that with young Flo.

You respected our womenfolk, didn't you, Jak? Jak with the flashy clan-ring and the hired puffwig leaning over the table at the babies' Ball, leering at me, man to man. You'd got it with a hot little piece your mate had introduced you to, hadn't you? All perfectly hushhush, outside the circle of cognate obligations.

You advised me to get it too. You even offered to fix it up with the self-same hot little piece—just tell the girls I had to stay late for some major memory inlays and the two of us would go out and have us some fun. She was a synaptic therapist you said, she knew her stuff.

I'll wager she did, Jak, a synaptic expert eh? Trust you to pick a specialist.

But I didn't go with you and you said I was scared. I said I loved Flo and Soo and Jin too much and that was something you'd never understand. But you understood, Jak, you understood.

Chariots, I was scared of your synaptician with her professional pleasure-center skills, shit scared.

§

Ben stood in the dust and the dust got into his boots.

An organic machine more virtuous than the hard variety, good frontier tradition, wholesome training for the rigors of eternal life, he ripped into the vines, and the juice ran down his forearms, sticky and sugary. Cuts and nicks scarred his fingers, nothing the ruth in his antibody-and-repair system couldn't heal overnight, and his hands were webbed with the cloying juice.

The tropic continent's sun burnt his neck and the skin peeled away. He sat in the shade with the other pickers and drank mock-tea and replayed his fiancée's letter, her sticky, sugary words. Dearest ben, just a short note to say how much i miss you.

And I thought I missed you. I even thought I missed Jak and Soo and Flo. But I left the Bjelke grapefields for Newstralia all the same, I didn't miss you that much.

In the bunk below Ben's the old ethyl-drinker cracked up in the night, shouting and laughing. They whispered that the old bugger was a ruth-immune, a social leper with his white hair and chapped skin, fated to die in a few years. Someone threw a bucket of water over him, but he shouted and raved regardless.

In the silent intervals Ben lay in his bunk and listened to the bloodsuckers whining through the pickers' shed—no insectivore screens for serfs—in search of their own brand of juice. Just as well they didn't pick up immortality with their supper, we'd be drowned in beating wings.

The next evening he called for his pay to be co-axed through to Creditbank, showered himself and hitch-hiked away towards the closest Teleport.

§

He ate a greasy shashlik on the durabond bench of an auto-cafe and walked out over the endless saltbush plains to the golden planet, Newstralia.

God knows what I expected in the place, it wasn't you, Jin, and it wasn't Jak's hot little synaptic therapist either. And it's not what I got.

The smart move would have been to wait in the diner for a lift, but he was footloose and happy enough to grab a chance to see some of another continent at close range. As he walked under the brilliant stars, thankful that this world possessed no predators larger than bloodsuckers, his library sent out the hitchhikers' radio bleat. Wouldn't do much good unless some compliant soul was tuned to it, but out here away from civilization they tended to do things like that.

Cargo vessels went overhead from time to time, their lights vivid in the empty reaches of the sky. But they would not set down for him in the night, and Ben was in no hurry.

Saltbush receded in choppy little waves to the black horizon. By most definitions this was hardly tropical territory, but it was warm for Victoria, locked down in glacial ice to forty degrees of latitude from its almost perpendicular poles.

He lay on top of his sleeping filament, resting his head on his rucksack, and looked at the familiar stars. In a day or two he'd be in another galaxy, a place so distant from here that it was only a smudge of stellar light. And his cognate kin would take him in, give him a month's free lodgings, introduce him around the warm, stifling company of Clan Griffith on Newstralia.

A domestic skite whistled low across the sky, its lights singeing the saltbush, bringing the clumps to a momentary blaze as the vehicle swept away, not stopping. Spread-eagled on the plain, Ben listened to the diminishing hum until the vast silence of the night reasserted itself.

He turned the bleep off and closed his eyes.

In the infinite gray-blue morning he stood and stretched, pissed on a handy saltbush, and reactivated the call.

§

He'd walked for three hours before anything appeared in the sky. A battered utility grumbled down, kicking up dust: in the sealed cabin, a man, a woman and a sleepy little girl. Ben shouted thanks and climbed up into the rear hold.

A woman clad in black sat on a duffle bag, her head a gleaming black inscrutable ovoid. Smooth, eyeless, a blind insect's skull. A sensory transduction helmet, Ben realized after a moment of almost instinctual terror in the face of the faceless maimed.

She moved a muse case to make room for Ben; it had a subversive symbol etched into it. Art transfiguring old political grievances, rendering them docile.

Her mouth smiled at him and, perhaps, her eyes as well. Her long black hair, hanging free from the back of the helmet, streamed in the wind as the ute lifted into the air.

Ben cleared his throat; allowing for the wind he spoke loudly, but the open cavern of the hold served to shelter his voice, so that his words came forced and nakedly nervous. "Hello." It caught in his throat, but he forced out some more words. "You hitching too?"

"As you see."

Shit, idiot, idiot! "Where to?"

"The Wagga Teleport."

His heart contracted in mad hope. What were the odds? One in billions? "For Newstralia?"

"Naturally. It's our cultural Athens, isn't it?" Perhaps she sniggered.

"I'm going there, too. Uh, I'm Ben."

"I'm Anla."

After a few more banal words they sat silent in the artificial wind, the day's early heat warming the ute's plast. By the time the farmer stopped in the broad common dropspace of a two-pub township the mirages had started.

Ben jumped down and took their baggage and the muse from Anla. He placed the instrument delicately but quickly on the grass, determined to offer Anla a hand down, but she had sprung out before he released the handle. The farmer's ute lurched away, and they went in search of breakfast.

It was still early and the wide common was almost deserted. Those few who were abroad looked at Anla, then at Ben, and back to Anla.

Ben was accustomed to passing unnoticed, insignificant, in any situation, even in piddling little country towns like this one. When he went out with Jin and the others nobody much looked at them, unless Jak was acting the lair. But they looked at this tall woman in her cruel mask, her tangled black hair, her muse and her duffle bag, and they looked at Ben with suspicion and envy. Her man.

They found an open commissary and waited interminably. The woman who was driving the floorwasher finished her task, took the plugs from her temples, and seared them a couple of eggs in rice.

Ben talked to Anla over the diamond-encrusted surface of the diner table. She was relaxed and friendly and more ready to communicate than in the hold of the ute. She'd been collecting scandalous folksongs around the island work camps; and finished up at Moroni the day before.

No, she didn't think it was very dangerous for a girl to travel alone. It was certainly a lot quicker. Ben felt an uneasy despondency. She'd want him to piss off after the snack.

But Anla talked easily and cheerfully about the rides she had got, the buzzes cargo pilots had bought her. They left the commissary and walked toward the end of the township, where the commercial vehicles landed.

"Do you want to travel alone?"

"No, of course not, unless you do."

She laughed at him. This girl dressed and masked in black, Ben thought with sudden joy, wants to travel with me.

§

And the first bitter, lonely ascent to the cold high place.

He'd been inducted through the special gates reserved for those who had never voyaged before, those innocents for whom the Teleport Authority had prepared interrogatory machines of peculiar thoroughness, jollity and avuncular tone.

Knocked halfway on his ear by soothing drugs, he'd gone into the maw of the Aorist Closure and dreamed away the pseudo-time of transition with fantasies of lust and childhood, and when he'd come out and pulled on his hired clothes he'd almost screamed with the pang of loss. He'd never see her again!

And the liquid relief when he'd stumbled out of the Men's Lounge into the principal metropolis of Newstralia, stretching away indifferent on every side, hostile in its indifference, and found Anla waiting for him, whistling and swinging one leg.

A woman from beyond the clan system. No rules to help, no norms of protocol. How can I ask her if I might see her again? He ran possible phrases over in his head, but before he could speak she said, "Where are you planning to stay, anyway?"

"Well, I'm Clan Griffith," he explained in confusion, "so I guess I'll phone the kin-center and get my room allotment...."

"Much better," she said firmly, "if you come and stay the night with my friends."

"Won't they mind?"

"No, they're our type."

What the hell are our type? Not clan-kin surely. Better not to ask, he decided, he'd find out soon enough.

§

Anla had credit enough for a cab; they flew to a precipitous series of terraces that fell away to the harbor. They walked down the hill to Anla's friend's place on El Cheapo Street.

A weakly-flickering holo on a downstairs window advertised an exhibition of pottery that had ended two months ago, if he had his date conversions right. A fellow with a thin goatee and an informal red ruff opened the door, embraced Anla, thumped Ben on the shoulder and showed them in.

The corridor was active with holos: for zam clubs, recondite feelies, acted drama, art exhibitions, semi-legal political rallies: a fey red fist wiggled its stiff thumb up imperialism's arse. Between the holos of one wall three doors stood at regular intervals. **Pandora's Jar** was stenciled in neat gothic script above one. Another advertised itself as **The Vatican**, whatever that might be.

They entered a room at the end of the passage; sunset lit, half a dozen people sat around vidding their libraries or simply doing nothing.

Gregorian chant.

Steam drifted across the room in puffs from the bright oblong of the kitchen door, dissolving in red gloom. A large, tortured, unframed painting on one wall confronted a creditable meme-copy of a primitive mask originated, no doubt, on one of the New Guinean worlds.

Anla appeared to know everybody in the room, introducing Ben with the speed of a racing commentator. Dazed, he sat on a huge transparent cushion next to a girl in a patchwork jacket who sat cross legged flicking up images from an expensive fashion program. He felt extraordinarily tired; the Authority's tranquilizers had not worn off. The strong, welling voices of the monks filled his head with the need for sleep. He tried to recall the names of the people he'd just met but could only manage that of the girl sitting next to him: Julia, the same as his sib.

He watched Anla talking to the man in the red ruff. She hadn't taken the glossy helmet off. In the dark room its perception augmentation doubtless gave her a subtle advantage. What would she look like without it? Beautiful, probably.

Chariots, he was tired. The monks echoed on, the wide reverberating spaces of their cathedral fitting uneasily into the cluttered room. The Christers were very big this year. Wasn't their god due to put in an appearance? Millenarian number, or was it next year? 4000, or 4001? He never kept up with such controversies. But then again, whose calendar did they employ in their reckoning? Orthoyears, one would imagine, hinged on Old Earth's paradigmatic round, so that definitely made this 4000. There were problems with simultaneity, of course.

The long, sad Latin words rose and fell; another couple entered the room; a girl came and went from the kitchen bearing bowls and sticks that she left piled on a low table. A flask of red wine circulated. So they have grapes on Newstralia too.

Ben passed it to Julia; he didn't have a glass and anyway he didn't like liquid intoxicants. He noticed Anla leave for the kitchen. She came back with a glass, filled it and handed it to him.

Knees to her chin she sat on the cushion, hands around her glass as if it were a fruit she was squeezing. Ben relaxed, happy to sip at the wine she had brought him, happy that she was content to sit silently beside him. The traumatic day had all but dehydrated him.

How many of these people actually lived here? It struck him

as a bizarre parody of the Clanhouse. The monks switched themselves off as the girl from the kitchen fetched a huge dish of curry to the table.

They ate more or less in silence. Red ruff, who had the air of chief inhabitant, finished his meal and made for the door. As he passed their cushion he said in a matter of fact tone, "There's a spare bed in the room on the stairs."

A bed, one bed. Did these people think he was sleeping with Anla? Should he explain that he'd only just met her? That would be best, he'd do that at the first opportunity.

No, better leave it to Anla, they were her friends.

Then, like a blow in the stomach: did Anla expect him to sleep with her, *to make love to her*?

He glanced sideways. Joking across the room with the girl who'd cooked the meal, she was finishing the last of her vegetable curry. How old was she? Without her eyes it was impossible to guess. A couple of years or a couple of centuries?

The really elderly ones sometimes went this way, he'd heard. Long past conscription to their Million, tired finally of the rigors of settling a raw untouched world and bearing children and building cities and starting industry and watching their kids and the kids of the kids of their kids booted out to open up other worlds again, they tore up their roots and became wanderers.

Exhaustion took him by the throat; he'd had about four hours sleep in the desert and then been hurled into circadian lurch. Could he plead tiredness and find some neutral place to lie down and sleep in? That would solve the problem of Anla as well.

But someone suggested a pub.

§

Suspended up here in the crystal clarity of Aorist no-time, he remembers walking in a group to the pub which stood in a mess of decaying plast domes and even older stone and durobond dwellings. Incredible noise. Anla buying him a buzz, him trying to pay for it, fumbling for his library. Very clearly he remembers Anla laughing at him. "Don't be so bloody clannish."

Did she mean obsessively responsible?

Lots of talk about somebody's exhibition and somebody's muse. Buzz synergized alcohol; unsteady on his feet he looked for somewhere to sit down; all occupied. Everyone standing and shouting at each other. He felt nauseated.

Everyone pouring at once, without warning, into the cool night air.

He recovered slightly; Anla had her arm around his waist. A skite fell from the sky. Sitting in the front with Anla on his lap, his arm around her, his hand on her thigh. The skite was overloaded with human flesh. The bubble was off and wind blew against his face.

Anla rested her head against his shoulder and the cool curve of her helmet pressed his cheek. He suddenly remembered something a mother had told him: drug addicts affected transduction helmets to disguise the fact that their eyeballs swell up. Or did they need them because their optic pathways had burnt out?

Chariots, she was a junkie! They were going to hear someone playing zam. Everyone knows zam players are all wireheads, it goes with the music.

He tried to reach up to wrench the thing off her head but she twisted in his lap and kissed him full on the mouth. Oh Jin! He felt startled and sick. She was sitting on his bladder and he wanted to piss.

They passed the scene of an accident: two crumpled skites embedded in a high rise roof. One rested upside down, its lift-coil in the air—a squat little animal, bloated in death.

It was impossible, didn't these maniacs use multiple autonomics? A stochastic universe: somewhere, eventually, even all the time, everything fails at once.

Lights pulsed: red from the cryoteam, blue from the cop skites.

Central routing took them past the catastrophe in a wide

curve, but Ben had time to see the frost-smoking vault of the ambulance close on a bright, clinical tableau.

§

They sat in the zam club drinking more alcohol. The discordant music was very loud, and heavy in the subsonics, and the olfaction specialist was a fat man with sweat running down his face.

And that is all he can remember, even in the chilled light of the Aorist Discontinuity. Memory proteins scrambled.

§

What happened that night? In the week that followed, and in the intervening years, Ben has often thought about it. Sometimes he's almost brought himself to ask Anla, but for some reason he has always remained silent.

I woke in bright sunlight. No polarization: it blasted my eyes.

Ben turned over. He was lying on a filament on a bare durobond floor in the incessant glare. He was naked. Someone lay next to him. She was naked as well.

Lenin, he was lying naked on a sleeping filament next to a naked woman!

He looked at her face; he'd never seen her before.

Yes he had, it was the girl he'd met yesterday, Anla, but without the sensory helmet. Holding his head in his hands, Ben groaned quietly to himself.

The girl Anla lay on the marble-veined inflated filament, dead to the world. He looked at her for some time, seeing through his nausea the way her breasts swelled slightly to each side. He put his hand over her near breast. It was much softer than he had expected, softer than Jin's or Soo's, but then he realized that there had always been, except for that ultimate grope, at least two layers of clothing between him and his fiancées.

Anla stirred and he felt her nipple fill under his palm. Then saliva was running down his throat and the contents of his stomach were rising to meet it.

The experience was unspeakably shocking. He had never been ill in his life, nor had anyone he'd ever met, except maybe the poor bloody ethyl-drinker with the ruth immunity. Ben got to his feet, almost fell over as the blood drained from his head, staggered and made it to the door.

He was on a landing—static stairs going up, stairs going down. He half fell down the stairs, blundered along the passage, guts heaving, degraded, charged through a room, through a kitchen and into the open air.

Again the sun blasting down, hotter than Victoria's glacial star. His whole body was betrayed by nausea and he threw up on the sparse brown grass. Some of it, bitter and stinging, went up his nose.

He fell to his knees, head in hands and guts spasming. For some minutes he knelt like that, eyes closed, the taste of yellow muck in his mouth.

When he knew that the final outflow was done, that his stomach contained nothing more, he crawled away and cowered, feeling slightly better. Ruth would heal it, but the repair process would take time.

Dully, he realized that he was naked. He forced himself to take stock: only the back garden. Not that he'd have cared much, truth be told, if it had been the middle of the People's Plaza.

A non-recyclable towel hung in the sunlight. He wrapped it around himself to cover his knowledge, and lay on the grass, a fallen innocent in a strange garden.

§

Or was I? Had I fucked Anla that night or was I so drunk I'd flaked out a virgin yet? Or had the wine, the tranks and fatigue rendered me impotent, the spirit but not the flesh?

§

Ben lay a long time in the garden. The sunlight seemed to lessen until it was just warmth defining the surface of his body. Still in red ruff, the man from last night found him, spoke gruff, friendly words of commiseration, and shot something into his neck. His skull was full of furious helium atoms. He slept.

The absence of pain in his head when he woke was the most beautiful thing he had ever felt. His guts had relaxed and he was hungry. Someone was playing soft muse. Ben listened to the chord changes; whoever it was lacked proficiency. He opened his eyes and Anla smiled her blind smile at him over the dazzling body of her instrument.

Despite the helmet, Ben thought he detected a gentle irony in her smile; it was hard to be sure, and it took a few seconds for the colors to come right in his blinking eyes. When she spoke it was softly-tenderly, he thought.

"Feeling better?"

"Much."

"Can I get you anything?"

"Wonderful."

"Coffee?"

"Thank you."

"A boiled egg? They only have nightingsnail spawn."

Even this failed to revive his nausea. "I'll try."

"Keep your eye on my axe." Anla rose slowly and walked towards the terrace. Sun in the leaves of a curious tree filtered through in a subdued, vagrant pattern. Anla returned with a pair of black, rubbery, glistening eggs, and two mugs of some hot beverage. It didn't taste much like coffee.

"What's the time?"

"Early afternoon, I imagine."

After a while he stood up and found his way back to the room's deflated filament, pulled on his hired garments over fresh paper underwear from a dispenser, and went back down to Anla.

They took a walk, demurely holding hands, and answered one another's questions. Ben was nineteen; he'd been at tertiary for a year, inlaying and educing data genetics. He planned to specialize in econics. He lived with his clan-kin, and was pledged to marry a handful of nonentities.

Anla, to his surprise, was only a year older. She was training to be an educer, and would finish next year. She did not live with her parents; indeed, strictly speaking, she had never had any. She was neither fucking nor not-fucking anyone in particular.

They both lived in Bolte, the major conurbation on Victoria. Anla said Bolte was the arse-hole of the universe. Ben said it probably wasn't as lively as Trantor, the world of her birth. Anla laughed. "A planet where puns are considered by law the highest form of human activity. It was founded by a Million under the philosophic guidance of that old poet, what's his name?"

Ben didn't have a clue. He had never even heard of the relevant galaxy.

"It's named after an imaginary place in some ancient poem the guy wrote." She shrugged.

Anla spoke of her clone, talking about him with a detached narrative air, as one might describe a well-meaning but slightly naive character in a play one had taken in some time ago.

Her clone had met her X-donor on Trantor during an Imperial guerrilla police action. Anla had been grown there. The woman had stayed when Jard was Millioned.

These days the deportation draft wasn't such a hassle, she said. Ben knew that much; a century ago they'd run out of authentic frontier worlds where you had to start from scratch. The entire universe's stock of Earthlike worlds was now settled by humans.

Her clone taught Language at the creative level, had composed a couple of huge Bankable poems in the eighties, and he'd been working on another one for the past fifteen orthoyears.

"It's about the fall of Estrildinae, he's been living the Trantor thing ever since," Anla said. "He left the Movement in eighty-seven of course."

Which Movement, Ben wondered, why in eighty-seven, who was Estrildinae?

§

In the bay a couple of dozen pleasure boats hung listlessly on magnetic beams, and further out a line of racing skiffs made the best use they could of the meager breezes available. Ben had never seen externally powered craft before, and the sight appalled him; it brought back images of the broken skites and the dead, frozen bodies.

A small park curved to the water. Anla and Ben sat on the grass, and his fears retreated. After a while they lay and kissed.

At the Arab restaurant Anla knew, she ordered highly spiced food they ate with their fingers. Ben wasn't sure that he liked it, but he said nothing. They walked back to the terrace through twilight; no one was home.

§

For the first time I can remember I made love. It was better than I'd imagined it would be, more sweat and smells, altogether more effort and less spiritual adventure.

Those cant words *spiritual adventure* had occupied an honored place in his private world. No longer.

For five days and nights (longer than on Victoria, and more exhausting) Anla and Ben did little more than wander amid alien familiarity and screw each other in the room off the landing. On the sixth day Anla teleported back to Bolte and Ben trudged to the Griffith ziggurat.

§

Aunts and uncles on detail fed him cakes and cookies and gave him a bed in the unmarried youths' dormitory, where the rough companionship was the same as ever and the odor of farts hung on the air and Anla was a galaxy away.

The front office arranged a seat at the all-live musical, and three sexless motherly souls rode with him up a lift-shaft to the top of a monstrous spire so that he might marvel at the splendor of the city below.

His new buddies pumped him for the dope on hot little pieces on Victoria and what your chances were, and offered to suck his cock on a turn and turn about basis, but he was through with all that, corroded inside.

Representatives of Clan Griffith expressed disappointment that he could stay on Newstralia only two days; there was, they assured him, much of an educational nature to see and do. They dispatched him to the Teleport in a clan skite, and charged him nothing for the entire treat. Families have to stick together, that's what they're for. None of this touched more than the surface of Ben's being. Soon he would be with her again.

Anla, Anla, Anla, oh Charioteers, Anla, I loved you then.

§

In Bolte, Ben had the tissues of his brain stuffed with more knowledge. He moved out of the Clanhouse and went to live with Anla. His parents all disowned him. Jin cried and said he had become a disgusting pervert. He was late getting his memetic bugs to breed and they mutated into nonsense. He asked Anla to marry him on a pair-bond basis. She laughed a lot but agreed quite happily, agreeing with Jin and finding the notion delightfully perverse.

Of Anla's friends the two he liked most, the ones they saw most frequently, were Theri and Kael, also at tertiary, also living *a deux*. Kael's parents were a troika, whom he described as "white liberals". Theri's were an unfashionable couple, bound by maniacal doctrinal tenets.

The threesome, medicos with a joint practice in one of the more affluent subzones, didn't exactly delight in their son spending his student days in co-habitation with Theri but certainly didn't object. "Heterosexuality is something you have to work out of your system," one of his fathers had told him tolerantly, and they backed their judgement by supplying him with generous handouts of credit to supplement his baby grant.

The sole source of friction was Kael's refusal to educe medicine, plainly the only possible road to status and professional security. They viewed the study of galactic history in much the same light as the study of basket weaving.

Taking no chances, though, they insisted on removing the operative portions of Theri's gonads and putting them on ice, a fact that would have incensed her Christer-revival tech father had he been capable of facing the fact that his daughter was living with Kael in the first place.

The fiction existed that Theri dwelled with two other girls in a purdah block (as she had done, in fact, for the first six weeks after leaving her nuclear nest). Her father never visited his daughter's alleged place of residence, run by a cynical old bird who took her exchange-value where she found it; there, uneasily, the matter rested.

Shortly after Ben and Anla had started living together, a few months before they were formally pair-bonded, all four had spent a couple of days with Anla's clone. Ben had been apprehensive about meeting Jard. Confronting the man with whose female replica you are living in sin was not, he told himself, everybody's idea of a merry outing.

When they reached Jard's home—a hundred klicks or so from Bolte and almost engulfed by the uncleared scrub that covered the side of the gully—there was Sofy, no older than Anla and talking about the baby she and Jard did, in fact, conceive almost two years later.

To Ben's surprise, Jard looked nothing like Anla; it would take months before he recognized that they looked exactly alike.

Jard's soirees were relaxed, languid and full of food and buzz. The indeterminate number of house guests drifted around between meals, occasionally extending themselves to scenic walks, or swimming in the creek at the bottom of the gully.

Jard had been pleased to see Anla, although he seemed to have little idea of what she'd been doing for the last three months. He wasn't sure if she was still taking inlays or had started educing others. He told Ben that if the Imperial guerrillas had been as well armed as the insurgents they would have won in half an orthoyear. Ben wasn't perfectly certain of the moral embedded in this estimate, or even which police action Jard had in mind. There were so many, bubbles in the stochastic stew.

On the first afternoon, Jard proposed building a bridge over the creek. There existed a perfectly serviceable series of stepping stones, but Jard thought a proper log bridge would be handy in times of flood.

They cut down the biggest tree they could find, taking turns with an underpowered laser, everyone having a go except Sofy, who had remained in the house.

Those not burning sat under the trees fixing. Jard had an unlimited supply of buzz. There was a lot of high-level discussion about the way the tree would eventually fall: people drawing diagrams on their libraries of tree-trunks with bits burnt out of them, calling up recondite functions, modeling vectors, making allowance for those movements in the top boughs attributable to the alien intelligent life-forms held by common agreement to be hiding from humanity on Victoria, and for any abrupt Milankovic reversals in the ice caps.

One of Jard's guests, a poet named Jacko, developed his own theory and started to burn the tree in a completely different place. He gave up after a few minutes and handed the laser to Theri who took it back to the original cut, using the beam like a photonic battering ram.

It took at least two hours to sever the thing. It fell in the only direction possible, following the big branch that jutted out halfway up the trunk. After a few minor branches had been trimmed from the log, Jard decreed that enough toil had been done for the day.

Kael the historian pointed out that by Homeworld reckoning the next day was Sunday, and Jard announced that it would be sacrilege to work.

"We will all have a day for the Consort."

"Don't tell me I've fallen among ardent imperialists." It was the first remark Ben had volunteered; he hoped it had the right spirit of outrageous banter. Jard put his hand on Ben's shoulder:

"The Empress of heaven, my dear Ben."

Odder still to have fallen among deists, but he didn't say anything.

§

Jard and Anla had their argument on "Sunday" night. Anla had told Ben that every time she saw her clone they had the argument. It was a family ritual, a reaffirmation of the para-sib bond or somesuch.

The argument was about ancient Russia. Anla held that life in Mother Russia had been no better than life today under the Universal Revived Leninist Imperium, which everyone agreed was not much chop. Jard said she didn't know what she was talking about. Anla called him a recidivist. Jard called her a halfbaked romantic. It was all very languid and friendly. A lot of buzz was shot.

Anla started on about Chomsky, the rebel planet where they were still trying anarchism in the face of Imperial objections, but Jard didn't appear to know very much about it. He said, though, that Noam was on to a good thing. Anla agreed with him.

§

For the first time he could remember, Ben was impotent. Anla consoled him in a rough, slightly incredulous manner and turned her back to him and went to sleep. When it happened the second night she swore, made Ben get dressed, and took him for a long walk. In the small light available he blundered through the bush after her, branches striking his face, fallen moldy logs tripping him up. Anla marched on, saying nothing. She led him by a circuitous route back to the house. As they passed Jard's skite—parked in a tumbledown shed by the side of the bush track—she suddenly opened the vehicle and pulled Ben inside. Plastic upholstery, and no Jak rapping too soon at the window.

He experienced a remarkable recovery of his powers.

§

They were pair-bonded by a sociobiologist, with the sanction of the Imperium and the laws of Victoria. All Ben's relatives were there in rebuke, and a motley collection of Anla's friends turned up. Ben's clan-kin appeared still to be in disbelieving shock, and his ex-fiancées wailed. Some of Anla's friends stood with raised clenched fists as the happy couple did a formal mating dance. The party afterwards was widely considered the best ever held. The groom collapsed in a dead stupor at four in the morning; the bride held out to 0530.

§

Three months later Ben realized that Anla was having an affair with one of the demonstrators in the Tachyon Institute, a man he had introduced her to at a party.

His wife defended herself by saying that it wasn't anything that you could call an affair—she doubted, in fact, if people had "affairs" these days—the demonstrator was far too dreary a man for that anyway, she'd just screwed him a few times because he was lonely and neurotic and in need of a boost to his ego. She presented the whole exercise as a slightly tedious act of charity.

Otherwise, life with Anla assumed the rigor of a fattening diet. She fed Ben script-codes, ideas, opinions, art exhibitions, avant garde feelies and friends in much the same way she served up his dinner. Finding that Ben had never heard of Warschauer, the fax would run hot with her poems. That done, *The Aesthetics of No-Time* or *The Zeitgeist Machine* or *Clone Symbologies* or *Discords VIII* would be presented for consumption.

And Ben vidded them all, and listened to the crystals, and argued with her friends, and overcame his prejudice against people who guerrilla the authorities and was almost arrested himself for singing a seditious song in a public place.

The only noticeable effect he had in return on Anla was that she abandoned her transduction helmet after he told her it looked adolescent. The muse languished of its own accord and was eventually turned in for credit.

§

A Clan moot, shocked into action by Flo's abrupt defection two months after the wedding, agreed on a motion taking cognizance of shifts in community attitudes, accepted Ben back into their collective bosom and periodically sent representatives round for tea.

On these occasions Ben was always uneasy. He would tidy the dwelling immaculately before their notified arrival and beg Anla not to swear while they were present. His feisty spouse would threaten to subject his kin to every obscenity she could lay her tongue to; in fact, her language remained a model of socialist respectability for as long as her kindred-in-law were in the house.

She plied them with tea and cakes she would purchase specially for the occasion, invariably the most revolting, sugary, bauble-encrusted abominations she could find. Once she brought out a pack of absorbent doilies with pastel-colored foddles impressed on them.

If she gave them coffee it was always synthetic, despite the fact that she had real beans in the kitchen. She maintained a flow of bright, amiable, mindless chatter. At no other times did Ben hear her talk like this.

I felt resentful but couldn't really say why. She was clearly sending my cognates up, but then I had rejected their values as well; why should Anla's satire worry me?

Sitting over my ersatz, I'd feel my antagonism rising equally toward wife and kin. Anla seemed to harbor no antagonism at all; in fact she appeared genuinely fond of the dads and uncles.

She would talk to them about the difficulty of keeping a lawn healthy with the ecology still in transition.

She discussed the ethnic enclave policy without shouting, agreeing with them that the one thing to avoid was the sort of situation that had developed on so many open Teleport worlds, with their riots and hatred. But, she would suggest modestly, surely the Victorians—with their reputation, famous throughout the Empire, for equality and calling a spade a spade—ought to set an example to the rest of the universe.

She proposed, in line with Imperial decrees, a civilization in which all races and sexes might live together in harmony and peace without discrimination based on tint, gender, creed or tongue.

It was all very cozy but Ben could hardly escape the feeling that not only was the whole performance an elaborate private joke but that the joke included him. When he mentioned this, Anla replied that if his Clan-kin couldn't understand her the least she could do was try to understand them.

By devious means she identified and singled out his biological parents (though his paternity was, in the nature of things, a trifle uncertain, and Ben put his foot down when she asked him to run a genescan for her information).

Her rapport with Ben's putative father increased with every meeting. She called him by his first name, Hari, and occasionally "mate" or even "cobber". He seemed delighted; rather, Ben thought, like a child who has finally been accepted for advanced inlays.

During one particularly convivial conversation Anla asked Hari if he fancied some buzz-dust in his coffee. To Ben's and his mum's surprise, the Griffith jovially agreed that endorphins in moderation were no bad thing. Ben could remember only twice seeing an uncle fixing before; both times it had been to celebrate a Clan espousal. Anla produced the stash and shot a good blast into Hari's cup, then her own. Ben's mother refused with the voice of an outraged rabbit. Ben declined.

Anla and her new relative got through three quarters of the

stash between 1630 and 1700 in the afternoon.

After that session the visits became less frequent, and alternative emissaries were detailed. When Hari did appear he was just as amiable, or seemed to be, but Ben thought his jokes and bonhomie a bit forced.

The mums and aunts talked mainly to Ben, favoring the outsider with bright, chilly smiles and, if obliged to address her, spoke patronizingly, using the tone Ben could recall from the playroom when one of the children had asked a question nobody could answer. Anla simply took to ignoring the Griffith women.

What Ben sensed without being able to pin it down was a new tension that existed between the sexes on these occasions. The air seemed to hum with it, at a pitch just beyond human hearing. Yet he knew it well: the holding frequency of stations temporarily shut down but ready to resume transmission the moment the possibility of third-party eavesdropping could be discounted.

At length the visiting roster once more threw together Hari and Ben's biological mother. Incredibly, Anla fetched out the buzz-dust again. Hari rather apologetically refused; it seemed he needed a clear head that evening. He glanced quickly at his spouse but she was fixing Anla with a wintry stare.

Even a casual onlooker could not have mistaken the two youthful couples as coevals.

Anla continued discussing the habits of babies. Hari said the feelie stars were to blame. Anla said that most feelie stars were all right but she had to admit that some of them led less than exemplary lives. Hari said that some of the kiddies emulating the behavior of these feelie stars were pre-pubescent. Anla said yes, that was a bit young to start. Hari wondered how they could have any respect for themselves, but Anla felt the trouble was that half these kid's nurturers hadn't got a clue about life and so were in no position to give thorough-going advice. Hari strongly denied that a universal community some of whose members were 2000 years old didn't know anything about life; to hear some of the babies today talking you would think they knew everything; you would think they had invented sex.

At explicit mention of this phenomenon, Ben's mother spilt her coffee.

Her eyes were bonded on her husband but Hari, who was talking somewhat faster than usual, looked only at Anla. And Anla looked back at Hari with an amused, interested and very slightly mocking smile, sipping her horrible drink with gentle, feline fastidiousness.

How, she wanted to know, could members of a Clan be well-informed about life? After all, most of them had dwelled in their ziggurats until they were Millioned, and then as soon as they could they started new ones. And most of the true oldsters were beaten down by their centuries of raw frontier-world deprivation, the immortal women laden by endless pregnancies.

Here Hari produced his trump: he had fought more than once in Imperial wars.

Ah yes, Anla had to admit, guerrilla war, where anything goes.

A roguish glint came to Hari's unwrinkled eye. He had been on recreation leave on Siderea Lux. Lux eh? Anla was visibly impressed.

At this stage Ben's mother stated loudly that it was time to leave, stood up, retrieved her towering hat—she had not taken her furs off—and all but frog-marched Hari out of the house.

§

In fury, Ben accused Anla of leading his progenitor on. Anla happily admitted this obvious fact, and went on to speculate that Hari had probably reached the high point of his sexual life on the rampage with his mates in some Luxian brothel.

This thought shocked Ben more than he cared to admit. The idea that Clan elders ever had sex with anyone at all was hard enough to credit. Presumably they must have done so once, and indeed must be compounding the offence—witness himself and his sister, and the fact that half the mothers were pregnant right now. No matter how many centuries old they were.

It did not occur to him for a long time, despite his coaching in psychodynamics, that this revulsion was the expression of an inlayed incest-aversion, a structured and calculated syndrome. You could see the sense in it, though. After all, in physical terms at least, his mothers and aunts were desirable, nubile women in the peak of bloom.

Still, this vision of his dads and uncles as drunken, whoring troopers, evoked so casually by Anla, unsettled him for days. And when Anla with equal nonchalance articulated what he had so valiantly repressed, that Hari's interest in her was basically carnal ("He thinks I'd be a good lay"), he was appalled.

Yet his anger was without focus: all that Anla said was probably true, was undoubtedly true, and Good Reason knew he was no disciple of his Clan's mealymouthed, soul-sapping respectability. Breaking out of that prison, that polished pyramid echoed and reechoed on a billion worlds beyond the Aorist Discontinuity—its wall to wall obsessions, its segregated apts, its babbling hollies—had been the best thing he'd ever done. If Anla had excoriated his cognates with the violence he himself sometimes felt, that wouldn't have mattered; it was this amused, tolerant acceptance and dismissal in the same breath he couldn't swallow, the private joke in her unhelmeted eyes as she handed those loathsome pink squares of cake around.

§

After the Siderea Lux episode, the Clan quit their pervert's nest for good. In the couple of years since, Hari had dropped in four times by himself. He always appeared uneasy and did not stay long. Ben had responded dutifully by going to tea at the ziggurat every few weeks, unaccompanied. At first he found going home alone ("going home"!) far more bearable than receiving rostered kin. This way he was meeting them on their own ground and Anla wasn't there to upset him. Jin and Soo and some new ones kissed him on the cheek, as a brother.

His biological mother took once more to attacking the way he and Anla lived, but he replied with spirit that this was the way they both liked to live and it was no longer the concern of anybody else.

The menfolk sided with his mother in such disputes, but Ben believed he held his own. The adrenalin of contempt tingled in his fingers, but the overall effect was cathartic—liberating, he felt sure.

He related a couple of these arguments to Anla. She wasn't impressed.

"What are you going to do when the women finally announce that basically you're all right, you're just being led astray by that black haired slut you've married?"

"She won't say that."

"Yes she will, Ben, and the rest will support her. That's what ghetto women always say about shiksa girls."

"You know it all, don't you."

"I know that much."

§

But the next time Ben sat at the high table his mother started to complain specifically about Anla.

"You can tell by the way the house isn't cleaned that she can't care less about our boy." A murmur of approval around the long table. "No woman can look after a man on her own, it's simply not natural. It mightn't be too bad at the moment but what's going to happen when you have children? It simply isn't natural."

Ben gazed into his soup bowl.

"Really, what sort of nurturer will Anla make? Babies need constant care and attention. They need cleanliness. There's no ruth for infants, never forget that. It is all very well for Anla to keep her home like a beast's pit if you can tolerate that, Ben, but a child's immune system—"

The harsh accent rising and falling. Other women chipped

in with agreement, corroboration and reprise, the men moodily spooned their soup.

Ben sat listening to his mother driving the wedge, denigrating Anla, every word confirming Anla's glib, confident assessment and prognosis. The woman really was amazingly pretty, he thought, looking at her clearly for the first time in his life. Why did she need to stoop to this?

Betrayed on all fronts.

And bloody old Hari—now that Anla wasn't actually present, crossing her long legs, smiling her cool, mocking, sexy smile—seemed to have lost his former regard for her. Weak-kneed bastard, currying a bit of cheap favor, as if the evil-tongued bitch couldn't do the job herself.

Maybe the whole performance would have had less effect on me if my relations with Anla had been smooth and secure. Surely I could have sat placidly through a thousand of these tirades secure in the knowledge that I would return to a warm, constant love. But the current escapade with the intern (successor to the tachyon demonstrator) was straining things almost to breaking point.

The whole thing was intolerable; he dropped his spoon with a clatter into the bowl, got up and walked out.

§

He went from the foyer into the lifeless, deserted public dropspace—any kids still up were sequestered in the playrooms—past the sickly, bespotted lawns, vivid hollylight spewing on to beds of repressed little shrubs.

He heard a Clan skite whining down from the roof, hovering level with him. Jak's voice came muffled from inside the vehicle. "I'll give you a lift, mate." Ben marched on.

Jak started to shout, telling him not to be a drongo, that he'd upset the elders.

I've upset *them!* Chariotfuckin*tears!*

A grass path led between two service structures adjacent

to the pyramid, barred to all but pedestrian traffic. I hesitated, turned toward the skite. Hari was sitting forward, silent, beside Jak. Violently, I swung away, crossed the dropspace and entered the lane.

The skite hesitated, then lifted angrily back to the roof.

§

I said nothing to Anla of this tribal invective, nor of the subsequent denunciations I learned to sit through in surly silence. Our life has continued after this fashion. *Hoo*ray fuck. Is my refusal to accept Anla's infidelities, as I accepted all her other values, simply fear of losing her? Without her, with the Clan a poisoned well behind me, who am I? What use her blase assurances that she doesn't mind if I, too, screw where I will?

He had swallowed everything else in the diet she prescribed. Why shouldn't the bill of fare include her sexual ethic? Why gag on this little morsel?

3.

And coming down out of the dark dark dark, the vacant interstellar spaces, the vacant, yeah, out of the vacant, falling out of the Empire's arsehole, the statesmen and the rulers and Ben. Victoria again. Home and work. And the Permanent Revolution.

The slide-field seized him and bore him into the light. A factory line of naked men. Catsize, still one jump ahead of him, turned and gave a cheerful wink. Ben found himself smiling. What did he really have to worry about, after all? Only the perpetual crisis of his marriage and the insurgent undermining of an absolutely entrenched empire.

Ben pursed his lips and whistled an illegal melody.

PART THREE

Theri jumped to the ground, waved thanks to her casual lift, picked her way through the drifting crowd to the pavement. Her hair blew past her eyes and she gathered it together, running her hand along the back of her neck, and tucked it under the collar of her fur. Cold night for seditious talk. She turned and walked quickly towards the Death Shop.

Ris was sitting gingerly on the radiation-hungry floor of her shop, right hand fighting a pitched battle with the Left Alternative.

Above the racks of defensive guns, holos of mortal heroes looked down, twice as large as death: geneborne eidetics of a score of recent Imperial actions. Thoroughly ambiguous works. There was nothing to tell the impartial observer which side you were cheering.

Ris glanced up as Theri entered the windowless shop. On the chilly surface the Alternative was fighting back, its teeth scraping the besieged wrist, little needle teeth going for the skygrey veins, raccoon ringed tail thrashing the floor. Ris stood up, scooping the Alternative from its battle ground and threw it across the shop.

The grundle gave a convulsive twist and homed in on Theri, all claws extended, found purchase on the vertical wall of her fur jacket and scrambled to her shoulder. Theri put her hand up and stroked the Alternative's filmy ears. An impression of gravel being shoveled into a bucket came from the grundle.

"Hello Ris, Kael here yet?"

"Underneath with Anla."

Theri propped on a container-cell table covered with phero-mone repellents. The Alternative jumped from her shoulder to the trestle, bounded to the floor and scuttled across the dense mat to ambush his half brother, Madam Brown, asleep on a stool. Madam Brown retaliated with spirit. The Alternative leapt for a display of force-filters and made a soaring bound to a shelf of sonic grenades. Madam Brown followed, centimeters behind. The Alternative came to an abrupt halt as the shelf ended in a solid upright, and turned, trapped with its tail to the wall. Madam Brown sprang: a fierceness of teeth and claws fell to the floor, together with a flat, blister-sealed spybeam heterodyner.

"All bundles out! Now!"

The animals made a dash for the door at the rear of the shop. Ris replaced the communications hazard and followed her grundles into the domestic realm.

Theri remained on the honeycombed table and considered the meeting scheduled in the cellar beneath her feet. She and Kael were, at best, fringe members of the Revolutionary Alliance, a group composed mainly of tertiaries, a few educers and junior academics, the entire "North Thing Street True Leninist Revolutionary Commune", and a couple of multicentenarians. The only enthusiastic member she and Kael knew well was Anla.

In private, Kael expressed a faint, slightly patronizing contempt for the narrowness of vision of the other militants. "What exactly do they think life would really be like in their postrevolutionary universe, what do they think the fall of the Empire would enable people to be?" he had asked Theri once.

Even more privately, Theri agreed that the cant of the militants lacked on the whole any undercurrent of human kindness and joy in life, but Kael's mothersmilk love of peace and quiet repelled her equally.

It was really only Anla, articulate and scornful, who seemed to Theri to combine anything approaching a genuine lust for the richness of life with a proper contempt for those who would smother life in its cradle. She envied Anla her fiery words as much as she resented the ease with which her friend slid into the bed of whoever wanted her.

Theri rarely spoke at these meetings although her attendance was far more regular than Kael's. When he did turn up, Kael would say his cool rational piece and leave early, walking home alone. She would return to their apt, having said nothing all evening, but full of political purpose, to find Kael vidding in bed and far more interested in talking about the latest quasar expedition than the creation of post-imperialist consciousness.

Sitting on the table of *faux*-weapons, Theri resolved to say something at the coming meeting, to clash with Anla, openly and publicly, if only for the good of her self-respect. Anla, after all, would be sure to say something debatable.

The bolt-door in the corner cycled slowly open and Anla, Kael and a couple of other fraternals emerged from the cellar. She joined their number, and they made for the Sinese-style restaurant around the corner.

§

They returned to find Catsize trying to sell a soft bomb to two yobos in wire trousers and simulated shrunken skulls. Ben, Ris and a few others were scattered around the shop, ostensibly examining armaments from the shelves.

"Listen, zinger, Unarmed Love Defense is recommended for centies who are either amputees or promiscuous, but soft detonation is where it's at when it comes to neo-transmortal transfiguration and the conservation of souls. Zinger, it's freezy." Catsize's voice was super-freezy. "It's on a lateral meaning-plane. It's sidewise, zinger, parallel."

The boy in blue wire looked doubtfully at the proffered sublethal and turned to his companion:

"Wha' d' yer reckon?"

Green wire reached over and took the bomb, armed it without enthusiasm. "What if it goes off by accident and hurts you?"

Catsize regarded him with amazement. "What, a dangerous bomb? Do you think the Imperial police would permit the free sale of anything so tasteless? No, my son, these weapons are all guaranteed hyperstable. See, it says here on the side, it can be activated only by the malicious EEG intention waves of a would-be assailant or traitor. The defense of the individual is the defense of the State, you know."

Green wire turned to blue wire:

"Wha' d' yer reckon?"

"Maybe we ought to ask the Oracle."

They bent over a library, looked up in dismay. "Hey, zing, what the fuck?"

Catsize glanced quickly at Ris, who shrugged.

"Sorry, zinger, the shop is shielded. What's your sign?"

"Taurus."

"Taurus eh? You wouldn't want to hesitate too long, zinger. Like things can get pretty nasty for Taurans that pissfart about. No bull, zing."

Anla groaned under her breath; Kael picked up a grundle and buried his face in its fur. Blue wire shot a suspicious glance around the shop, catching the half-controlled grins.

"Yeah, well, we'll access the Oracle someplace else, zing."

"You do that, zotter." Catsize conceded defeat, taking the bomb back and disarming it. He added a contemplative parting shot: "I knew a Taurus who pissfarted around once...he's in cryo, now, freezy Deadsville."

The two uneasy customers left the toy shop, mumbling good-byes. Catsize gave the sub-lethal back to Ris:

"What we need in this place are a few skulls and body-skis and good-luck charms, instead of all these psychodynamically approved hostility vectors. Frankly, I thought they looked a bit old for this sort of thing anyway."

§

After Theri and the others had gone down into the cellar,

and Catsize had made off on some private mission, Kael sat by himself for a while in Ris's living area.

Painstakingly, he sought the pressure seams on a mobile energy gun. Its packaging declared it a ninety thousand cycle unit, fitted with the standard ethical circuits permitting it to fire only in self defense.

A tantalizing problem in volitional psychology, that. How would such a thing be proof against a sociopath or, say, the generalized pre-emptive attack of self-protective paranoia? His fingers probed at its barrel without conscious direction.

More to the point, why do the Imperial psychodynamicians consider such a sales pitch desirable in hostility toys?

Surely the aim was to cathartize improper impulses through fantasized enactment. And most violent impulses were improper precisely in the degree to which you wished to inflict undeserved punishment on the innocent, or at any rate to act aggressively beyond the limits established socially as your role.

So the rubric constituted a piece of denial, of repression, embedded in the very tool of displacement. Hardly made much sense, on the face of it.

There was a tiny click; the toy's indicator lights died, and Kael's fingers found a crevice in the plast surface.

That was the point, though, wasn't it: none of these vectors were self-evident until you'd studied the field in depth. Manipulative psychology was simply too vast, its principles too arcane, to find expression in intuitively satisfying tags and slogans.

The toy slipped apart with a dry pop. Its molded hull was hollow. Oh you fools, I know $e = mc^2$, but you've left the m out. I'm a dead duck.

Voices rose from the open bolt-door, arguing as usual over priorities and first principles. Kael stopped sniggering at his own joke and rested his head tiredly on his arms.

Why had he bothered to come? To keep Theri company? To prove something to Anla? Because of some genuine conviction?

I have a passionate concern for freedom, he told himself, but the Revolutionary Alliance hardly seems the tool for battering down the Empire's colossal gates. If we counted for anything they would have closed us down long ago, dispersed us to planets right across the sky. Not for the first time it occurred to Kael that the local authorities tolerated meetings of this kind on the same grounds that they encouraged the sale of hostility toys. Yet that was the final gamble one must take: that freedom was not wholly gone, that thought and action were not utterly impotent.

Listen to the silly buggers. How much history do any of them know?

Lonek has been through the fire, but did the horror of confrontation leave him with anything more than trauma, desperate courage and a good deal more respect for the enemy than the rest can muster?

Kael's mouth moved in self-irony. My training as an educer has made a prig of me.

He did not really believe that.

He sat up and began reassembling the energy gun. Putting the toy together again was more difficult than taking it apart. How do you take an Empire apart? A trillion trillion feedbacks, incomprehensibly redundant, self-rectifying, updating itself on the basis of mutating bug projections.

I'd start by giving these buggers a lecture on how we got where we are. All they have, most of them, is post-adolescent misery and scraps of ideology. Their heads are stuffed with data-peptides and no one is asking them the right questions to get the facts out and structured into consciousness. Put any number of discrete inquiries to them and the figures'll pop out, but they add them together with all the dexterity and intellectual command of infants juggling bright blocks.

Kael pulled out his library and did some sums. Well folks, it's now 3528 orthoyears since the fall of the Roman Empire, if you count the transfer of formal sovereignty from west to east as the clincher. Stout work, Odoacer.

The British Empire fell apart 2057 years ago, and the Russian

Empire got the *coup de grâce* 2015 years back. Then there were the Americans and the Sinese and the Nihonese and so forth.

Fell my arse. Civilizations transform, they don't fall.

Technology and ecology corrode them, inflation and taxes and military adventures and polygenic infusions warp and buckle their structures, macromemes mutate and radiate explosively, classes rise to pre-eminence and their power wanes, and the only way to graph it all is on parameters of your own choosing. Flip the axes through 180 degrees and change the signs and a pitiable decline becomes a heartening climb.

Is that all bullshit? Liberty is the only yardstick: autonomy for the individual and his or her chosen affinity group.

Sophomore ethics—is the starving, uneducated freeman freer than the well-fed, cultivated slave? The bushman in his multiplex, stationary society or the wage-earner trapped to narrow skills in a tremendous high-energy culture?

Members of the Revolutionary Alliance: We live and have our immortal being in a stupefyingly complex civilization born from the dialectic collision of two realities—a technocratic order incapable of coping with the consequences of exponential growth, and the Aorist Closure, gift of the unknowable Charioteers.

You there with the gold hair: what was the first impact of the opening of the Teleport Gates?

Uh, all the dissidents and special interest affiliates and competing nations and all that pissed off, didn't they? Grabbed their piece of real-estate in the sky and sought the meaning of freedom after their own lights?

Wrong! Check his peptide stock, doctor, I think the memory molecules must be destabilizing.

But sensei, isn't that what we learned in civic—

Very likely, but if you'd think a bit instead of vomiting up the glib drivel they pump in, you'd see the holes in that little fairy tale in about a minute and a half. And aren't you forgetting our little fuzzy friends?

Our little- Oh, you mean foddles. The longevity drug! Oh

well, if it hadn't been for the Charioteers leaving foddles scat-
tered from hell to breakfast I don't suppose we'd have developed
immortality with the technol—

Exactly. The Diaspora would have gone ahead, because
those people were choking on their own garbage, but it would
have been conducted as a fascist operation only one degree less
appalling than global nuclear war.

But sensei, I thought you were arguing against *the Empire?*

Indeed I am, but there are levels of coercion. With the isolation of the ruth antimorts, people could be bribed to leave Earth
for worlds lacking even the most primitive elements of civilization. Had the Aorist Closure permitted the transportation of
anything but mammals high up the phylogenetic tree, matters
might have been even more liberal.

It was obvious that Earth would be the industrial base to the
universe for centuries, before the first colonies got from root-
grubbing to integrated circuits, but the prohibition on trans-
porting armed troops insured that central control got structured
in right from the word go.

Sensei, you've lost me.

All right, my dear, I'll try not to tax your tiny brain too much.

You don't talk like that to the girls.

Look, Fred, just keep your ears wide and your mouth sealed.

Kael shook his head in the empty room. This was no way for
a diploma'd educer to conduct a fantasy. *Draw* the knowledge
out, *show* don't *tell*, and so forth.

As usual, the complexity of it all defeated him. He doodled
on his library, sketching flow charts and expunging them as
the lines looped into meaningless scribble. The voices from the
boltdoor were droning on.

Where the hell did you start? With "human nature"? The
drive-to-power of authoritarian personalities?

Neither of these, for they were contingent, mutable before the
demands of each culture. It wasn't that certain men or women
were obsessed innately by the lure of outrageous authority;
rather, technologically stratified cultures *required* it. Tribal

hunter-gatherers had the same genes, but, since disproportionate power could serve no end, those with a lust for it were contained by their peers.

Should you start, then, with the imperatives of technology?

Certainly the ruling elites and their advisers had been quick off the mark, all those long twenty centuries ago. Lacking memetic analog proleptics, they had possessed nevertheless the formidable instruments of linear programming, catastrophe and complexity theory, hard computers capable of running elementary trends. Resource scarcity had already hurled them into supranational rationality, the long view of technological monopoly.

When the Aorist Closures had been found, they had seen swiftly enough that the flight to freedom could not be countenanced.

Let the last Aborigines of central Australia pass naked to the world of their choice, *en masse*, and that world was lost to technological civilization. No matter that worlds beyond counting waited out there: in a few thousand years they would be filled, and the Dreamtime planet would have been long since barricaded. The poisoned flour and diseased blankets of an earlier century's empire could no longer be relied upon, because the appalling mechanism of the Closure edited out the viruses carried by its passengers.

And thank Good Reason for that! It could hardly be otherwise, of course. Kael's mind cringed, briefly imaging a universe of slightly differing ecologies, each world with its feculent viral and bacterial pests linked by virtually instantaneous doorways. No inbuilt barrier to disease. Cosmic epidemic.

Some specialists theorized that the Charioteers had perished that way, slain by some gene-embedded virus too subtle for even their puissant defenses. If it ever happened to humanity, those theorists would have little time to enjoy the validation of their conjecture.

Yet those ancient bureaucrats, two millennia ago, had foreseen all this; it was difficult not to admire them.

An army could penetrate a world's perimeters, but it would be an army barehanded and bare arsed. If weapons awaited them at their destination, yes.... Guerrilla warfare, covert munitions works.

Viruses could be carried, but only in fragmentary form, coded as introns into genes by sculptors, neutral and harmless until respliced and reborn in a genomics laboratory.

A world of several million tribal Aboriginals, deliberately and coolly eschewing machines, barren of laboratories, could be defended by a ring of fire and spears around each Aorist locus. To the bureaucrats and their wealthy masters, that possibility was intolerable and abhorrent; when the Earth's population was bribed to the stars with immortality, it went in fragments of fragments.

Each Million held a hundred or a thousand dissidents, families shattered from their tribes, ideologists thrown among their enemies. And in the back-breaking labor of opening a universe, the seeds of autonomy were smashed, ten thousand years of history obliterated.

New coalitions had emerged, of course: the Clans, linking real and imagined heraldries in a fraternal masonry of trans-galactic scale. Others, defused by overlays of real and imposed memory, had been permitted to reform.

Kael listened to the muffled strine twangs of the conspirators, and smiled. A billion stellar systems traced their ancestry to Old Australia, a hundred billion to Old China. But the ties were notional, abstract as the beasts you could see in clouds.

So in the end it was the Closure itself that stood out as the principal determinant of human history.

It passed bodies and the information in their heads, or encrypted and coded into their genes. A single world's economy, founded on resource predation and the imposition of armed and financial might, discovered itself hurled into a constricted dimension where the sole transferable commodity was skill. Embodied information.

Instead of becoming the center of industrial imperialism,

Earth rose victorious as a mogul of data, information storage and processing, the scientific wellspring for the basic low-energy technologies which the new worlds needed before they could clamber up to takeoff.

The key to the universe, Kael told himself wryly, is not mc^2 it's $\log_2 N$. Ergs have given way to bits.

The Empire, he thought bitterly, is the apotheosis of bureaucracy, cybernetic networks as their own justification. Its bearers have power, and honor, and more sensual gratification than they can shake a stick at, but theirs is not an imperialism of rapine or chauvinistic glory. It's a universe made safe for science.

§

Theri moved her stiff shoulders against the cellar wall. Kael was nowhere to be seen. The voice of reason must have packed up and gone home, she thought irritably.

Well, maybe you can't blame him, this lot haven't been too elevated tonight. She glanced at the pair of newcomers sitting in the far corner. What do they make of it?

Anla had identified the black-haired boy when he came into the Death Shop, arm around the tubby red-haired girl. A pre-graduate from Curringal Basic Inlay—Con something or other.

The randomizer had elected Dav as chair. Self-confident and watchful, the boy listened to him make his dogmatic assertions. The girl looked sideways at Con as if seeking confirmation of some point Dav was making. The boy caught her eye, shrugged noncommittally.

Theri felt herself grimace. Dav was the prize example of Kael's unsubtle visionless militant, one had to grant that much, and anyway his hair was so moldy, like tangled-up steel wool. Self-inflicted ugliness in the cause of morale-building social rejection.

"Look, Dav, you listen to me." Fed up, Lonek rose slowly to his feet: the only multi-centenarian in the cellar, faded tartan jacket splotched with old oil-stains, belly locked in a trial of strength with the waist of his kilt.

Theri leaned back against the chilly spybeam-proof lining of the cellar and her eyes went involuntarily to Lonek's left sleeve. Hidden by the tartan crisscross the hypnotic little biofluorescent numbers would be riding the tendons of his forearm.

The sudden guilt of the spectator was sour in her mouth. She swallowed quickly.

"The one thing that truly frightens people is death," Lonek was saying. "Don't talk to me about the consciousness of toilers, Dav. When we run those freighters out to the gas giants I talk to the real toilers every day, the men and women whose own lives hang on the thread of Imperial technology. They don't talk much about autonomy, Dav, but they're the closest to free human beings we're likely to see until the new order is realized. They don't like the prospects of being Millioned, so they've opted for the tough dangerous jobs that earn them exemption. And I've never heard one of them speak kindly of the military draft, or of the police actions on planets no one's ever heard of except some data core on Earth. But I'll tell you this, Dav," he said more loudly, pressing over the attempted interruption, "every day I hear the same thing. 'I've got a daughter fighting on Kurd.' 'My great-grand dad's been called up.' 'My best mate is on Unilever.' And every day they tell me, 'We'll do anything to help bring the troops back from MacGregor and Rezakhan and Lomwe and Malagasy and a thousand other bloodbaths, but if you take one step that will stop them from getting out alive we'll dump you into space.'"

The cellar was utterly silent. Theri shivered, hugged her arms against herself.

"Do you imagine it's any different for the people who work here in the munitions autofactories? They know they're preparing stockpiles that could someday be used against themselves. Or the specialists who train the guerrillas, and those who code the viruses, and the ones who write the peptide-addresses that get the troops to those wretched worlds? When the Legates arrive here, Dav, the people who flock to the Teleports won't be in any loyal, flag-waving mood." He paused, shook his head in tired anger. "But let me assure you: if you want to guarantee the contempt and anger of every one of them, aimed right at your thick head, there's just one thing you need to do—threaten their fighting kin."

Dav seemed to have calmed down a little during the centenarian's weary outburst. "But Lonek, this is precisely the sort of ethnism the Empire depends on." In a parodic tone he said: "'These police actions will save Victorian lives.' Or wherever the hell your family happens to be clustered at the time."

"It might have elements of ethnism, friend, but people everywhere think their own kind are more valuable than foreigners they've never heard of."

"Which is just the sort of thinking that revolutionary autonomism is meant to be struggling against. I tell you, the only course open to us—"

A lanky technician, looking pained, cut in: "But as I keep saying, it's a matter of tactics. Lonek's right, we—it—"

"Well, if it's bloody tactics you're after, Mart," cried the chair, "just tell me what the tactics are for mobilizing opinion against the imperialists if we're meant to continually refrain from expressing any solidarity with the Empire's valiant dissidents because we don't want to offend the people we're trying to convince by saying what it is we're trying to do because if we come out in favor of the rebels we'll be alienating the false consciousness of...because...because...what are the tactics for that, Mart, what are the tactics for—"

"Belt up, Dav, you're raving." Anla spoke *sotto voce*, from her commanding position perched on the fax-output. Everyone laughed. Dav spluttered to a halt, grinned slightly self-consciously and started again.

"What I want to know is what is the point of—"

"What you want to know is when to shut up."

Dav reddened, gaped at her.

"Now you just listen to me." She swung one booted leg. Con's gaze, Theri noted with amusement, followed its arc. "When the

Imperial Legates come in from Earth in several weeks' time, we'll have an opportunity handed to us that comes maybe once in fifty years. Are we going to seize that chance or sit on our arses theorizing? Our sole reason for being here is, tactically, to resist completely the prosecution of all current Imperial police actions and, strategically, to prepare the ground for the revolution that will make such wars impossible. And the thing to fight is the mega-society that compels such murders, which means first Imperial Earth and second the Victorians on this planet. But some of you don't wish to offend public sentiment by creating a little havoc in the midst of the society that helps burn and poison our insurgent kin. Well, this is the most impotent bullshit I've yet heard around here. If it represents the boldest libertarian thought on Victoria we might as well all troop down and join the Imperial diplomatic service."

Theri watched Anla, cross-legged on the fax, and envied her scornful words. A single, heavy gold earring gleamed against the black mass of her hair; one arm lay languidly over the dumb bulk of the machine. Theri knew perfectly well that Anla had chosen the fax to give herself just the advantage of height, yet in no way did the premeditation lessen the effect.

The silence lasted a few seconds; then Kael's voice came dryly from above them:

"You haven't actually suggested any real course of action yet, Anla."

He had come quietly to the top of the stairs, the light from the open bolt-door immediately above his head illuminating the periphery of his hair. His features were almost indistinguishable. Anla had to turn and crane her neck to see him. She looked at Kael for a second and then turned back to the rest of the meeting.

"It's obvious. Attack the Legates."

It should have been ringingly impressive. But if her words had the substance of a battle cry, their effect seemed curiously diluted. Theri sensed Anla's unease at Kael's somber presence perched a meter above her head. Her words seemed to defy not so much the Empire's agents of coercion as those present in the cellar. A few more seconds of silence; the assembly waited for Kael to speak again. He said nothing. Dav, who had remained mute during Anla's attack, found a chance of revival; he spoke peevishly:

"There's only one chance in one hundred and twenty-eight that they'll come out at the Bolte Teleport, you know what indeterminacy does over distances of twenty-five billion light years, and anyway the facilities will be swarming with militia. Our job is—"

Anla spun to face him, and the room crackled. Kael might be able to upstage her, but not Dav.

"For fuck's *sake*, it doesn't matter how much real damage we do, or whether a Legate actually gets hurt. What counts is getting it through to Earth that its facilities, even in good old pacified Victoria, aren't safe from attack. And a repressive response can only have the effect of radicalizing more and more people who would otherwise be snug in their false comfort. It might not be the start of the insurrection but it's the most significant input we can provide at the moment."

Kael started to edge his way clumsily down the steps, bumping one step at a time on his buttocks. His face jolted into focus. He stopped almost level with Anla and a little to one side of her. Theri leaned forward quickly and started to say, "We shouldn't assume—"

Kael's considered opinion came gently from halfway up the steps, easily over-riding Theri's hesitant start. "It all boils down to the question of whether the short term issue of combating Victoria's involvement in specific current police actions is compatible with the long term objective of creating a revolutionary libertarian situation on this planet, and if not, which has priority?"

Theri sat back. Had he heard her start to speak? If so, had it occurred to him, even for a moment, to defer to her?

The muscles of her back ached. She listened to Kael expounding: quiet, sensible man defining the parameters of a revolutionary situation. The professional educer, drawing out what we all know and structuring it after his own perspective.

Material cannot be teleported through the Aorist Closure so the Empire must needs establish its armaments mechfabs on each separate world, each at its achieved level of technology. But its troops must come from outside, so the munitions works must be built around one or more of a planet's Closures.

To minimize the chances of successful attempts to enter such factories by means other than teleportation, they are located at Closures in arctic, inhospitable latitudes.

Hence, effective insurgencies must be well-rooted in specific, extensive local grievances and supremely equipped for blitz-krieg against the munitions fortresses. Harassing a handful of plenipotentiaries from Earth on a state visit to open Parliament hardly constituted the focus for an armed uprising.

Hmm. Can't really see you at the barricades, Kael. Still, you seem convinced it's a long way off. Just as well, eh? Not really a man for the lethal gas and the flare of gigawatt lasers. Not with immortality at stake.

But that's your dilemma, isn't it, Socrates? If the blood and guts spread around in a revolution are obscene, so are the rotting bodies on Kurd and Lomwe. Either way it's the ultimate obscenity in a universe of ruth immortality.

Behind your cool, rational analysis, Kael, you're making an emotional plea for parliamentary action—change society, boot out the Empire, all without bloodshed. Fine civilized values, Kael, my love; you're the only person I know who could make them sound so gutless and sensible in the same speech.

It just so happens, does it, that in promoting the distant liberation of Victoria we're prolonging the star wars and so, albeit most reluctantly, we'll just have to cool it for the time being and maybe get around to the revolutionary thing in a millennium or two?

And here's Anla bouncing back, saying what I'd say if I had her presence, accusing you of trying to have it both ways. Yet she's wrong, of course, just as I would be wrong if I were saying it. The battles on Rezakhan and MacGregor and Kurd will be over long before there's anarchy on Victoria, let alone Earth.

She saw Ris untangle herself from her seat in the center of the cellar and pick her way towards the stairs, edging up past Kael.

Theri followed her up to Shop level, inadvertently stepping heavily on Kael's hand as she passed him.

§

A grundle dozed in a high place, ears glistening like folded insect wings. Outside, the scheduled night rains were falling.

She scooped up the surprised Madam Brown and turned into the kitchen, where Ris was banging about with urn and mugs. The grundle started its industrialsound effects between her breasts. It was a relief; she felt nauseated with the sound of human voices.

§

There was no gain in continuing the debate, and besides, Ris would be coming down again in a few minutes with coffee for the conspirators. Thirsty work, overthrowing Empires. Rubbing his bruised hand, Kael went back up the steps. No Theri.

"She's gone, I think. Do you want coffee?"

"Oh. No, thanks, Ris. Say good night to the bundles for me."

"See ya."

In the thin drizzle, Theri was nowhere to be seen. Probably bleeped a hitch. Kael decided to walk home, as usual, head thrust forward into the falling mist.

A vague excitement of abstract dispute was still upon him. The world disclosed its multiplexed connections, humming with power, no single part of it unrelated to the rest.

Personal safety, he thought, is predicated on impersonal surveillance. In a world where people genuinely cared for one another, it'd be possible to hitch-hike without mutual guarantees of safe conduct. Today, the issues of benevolence and personality have been transcended by the machines; technology gives us the benefits of community without the moral contact, the risk of disclosure. Possibilities for good and ill have been foreclosed.

You punch your destination into the hitching system, the cybernet locates a bunch of commuters or cargo-vehicles going your way, one of their pilots responds to your call, you chat if you feel like it, get out, off it flies. If some psychopath fancies your coat or your body and proceeds with a quick essay in molestation, the cybernet has all the details set up in core. Crime does not pay.

Gusts of winter wind tore at Kael's hair; he squinted into the rain, hands deep in his pockets.

Something had made her angry. Last time this had happened they'd been coming home from her awful parents' place. Jesus of Nazareth in his shrine: the gold sphere resting in punctured hand, the other pointing to his pulsing, levitated heart, dripping blood, torn by vicious plaits of thorns. It seemed unlikely that the original Hebrew gentleman had green skin and blood-drenched tendrils. Theri had raved her blasphemies; the loon parents had glowered in the flickering fight of their barbaric icon. Theri and Kael had walked away from the place, eventually, to the public drop-space, her arm firmly around his waist. They'd trod the squares of a children's chalked hop-scotch game. On the glaze of a retail fuel-cell recharger faint words were scratched: *Beddoe loves Corris*. Kael had spoken quietly: "You lose your cool with your father, don't you?"

"Bloody halfwit."

"Why don't you talk to him rationally, it's useless to let him needle you like that."

"What would that old bigot know about anything, he's so fucking stupid."

"So are you when you talk to him, you carry on like an articulate cretin."

"Well why don't you ever bloody say anything if you're so bloody clever?" she'd cried. "Every bloody time we go round there you sit on your chair like a tongue-tied...like a tongue-tied—"

"—mentally defective genetic disorder in a catatonic trance?"

"Yes, fuck you, that's just how you look, sitting there staring at those hideous saints as if they were bloody works of art. And there's no need to look so fucking smug just because you're better at dreaming up invective than I am. At least I open my mouth and don't just sit—"

"It's about the only bloody time you do open your mouth, isn't it?"

"What?"

"You never talk at the Alliance meetings you're so fond of attending. You never argue constructively with me or Anla or the rest of us. You come back from tertiary complaining about the dreary tutorials, but have you actually said anything yourself to liven them up? No, because everyone else was being so dreary it was beneath your dignity to open your highly intelligent gob. The only time you get round to committing yourself is when you're abusing your dumb bloody father. And then you talk like an imbecile. You ought to learn to argue constructively, and to exercise a bit more restraint and charity with—"

"You...you...you're becoming a real bloody fourteen carat gold educer, Kael, aren't you? So you've condescended to read me a little homily so that I can rectify such defects in my character as you, in your wisdom, have seen fit to...to call to my attention? That's really very good of you, Kael, how would you like me to expiate my sins? A whipping in front of the shrine like that arsehole back there? Sanctimonious gutless bloody pig!"

"Who, me or your father?"

"Both of you, fuck you, I'm sick to tears of having my life ordered by pompous, self-righteous deadshits.... Fuck *me*! 'Restraint and charity' and lectures on character improvement! Don't touch me. Don't you dare touch me!"

Kael released Theri's shoulders from his tentative embrace; she spun on her heel and marched off, savagely punching a bleeper code on her library. She got it wrong and cursed and started again. Kael ran after her.

"Theri, I'm sorry, I didn't mean to sound so—"

"Oh Christ, so now you'll get all contrite and conciliatory so you can win me back to your...to your soft little peptide world where everyone is so sane and sensible, just how you'd like them to be, and nobody upsets you because they all behave as you'd like them to behave."

Theri had sniffed, suddenly, violently. She was going to cry. A man with a pet on a leash walked toward them, staring at Theri as he passed, smug half-concealed glee on his face. Nothing like a domestic scene in the common to liven up a drab evening. Kael felt like punching the man's head in.

A commuter's skite had dropped down to the common. Theri stepped quickly across the grass, holding up her winking library. Kael thought he recognized the same smug, vicarious grin on the half-seen pilot's lips.

Theri clambered in; she twisted into a spare web, looking at the far side of the common, her hair completely shielding her face. The skite rose swiftly, its lift-coil glowing, and re-entered its flight corridor.

Kael had started to tear at the grass with his toe. Instead, he'd sworn and begun to walk home alone.

§

Thinking about that episode now, trudging through rain and wind, Kael suddenly recalled the moment when Theri had started to speak in the meeting. Had he stifled her, cut her off, at the very moment when she needed encouragement most?

But the dialectic of the meeting had been poised at a delicate turning. It had been necessary to place Anla's simplistic emotional challenge in some sore of realistic perspective.

Ah, fuck it. Fuck it all.

§

He was awake, lying in their squeaking bed, when Theri arrived at 0300 in the morning. She entered the bedroom without activating the lights. Kael heard her taking her heavy clothes off, quickly but without haste. She slid into bed and lay with her back to him.

"Where have you been?"

"You could have asked my library."

"Yes, but I didn't."

"Talking to Catsize."

Her voice was friendly and relaxed. Kael put a hand on her shoulder. She resisted the pressure for a second, then turned quickly, kissed him on his mouth and returned to her original position.

"I'll screw you in the morning, Kael, go to sleep."

She was still asleep when he left the apt, with Anla, for Curringal Basic Inlay. An ambiguous entry to the real world.

PART FOUR

1.

Kael slumped in the passenger web. The ruffles around his neck choked him. He loosened the ludicrous ornamentation slightly but it was his blouse that was too tight.

Anla went manual and jumped lanes. She flew the skite with skilful arrogance, knowing perfectly well that the failsafes were in order; she'd run the diagnostic herself. Anla the competent, taking me high through the morning's traffic to the fields of gainful employment.

Commuter man now. Times for the rising. Times for the breaking or the gloomy continuance of my fast. Time bracketed by the autonomics of the Department's Big Board.

"Are you with the Department?" the little girl at the orientation dance had asked him. "So am I, I'm going to inlay the History of Ideas."

So were we all, dear, a whole 1400 days to cover five thousand years, a fair whack of thoughts per unit day. Fresh from the teaching machines to the peptide pumps, to the brave new tertiary arenas of durobond and force-field, with baby-grant credit to sustain us in our unfolding.

And so here we are, little girl. Are you, now suitably qualified, hurrying to some ghastly crèche the like of which you had only just left that night four years ago? Presumably not, since I didn't see you around after the Poststructuralist Heresies.

Got a menial job, or pregnant, went mad, choked to death

while overshooting in the Aorist Closure, living on a bureau-crat's wirehead asteroid in the Crab Nebula, who knows? I could trace your name and code on my library and give you a surprise call, but who can be bothered with additional lunacy at a moment like this?

Instead: tell me, Anla, hard at the controls, educer of two years standing, card spindling member of the Revolutionary Alliance, haranguer of hole-in-corner meetings, not a woman to make a foolish move outside the bedroom, tell me, does it fulfil your life, this Socratizing?

Aye, we've heard tell of them, haven't we, the few with their wits still about them, fresh with enlightened inlays, eager to destroy the dragons of innate and conditioned stupidity. If the system is oppressive, all the more to fight.

A hundred days, two hundred, a year and the fight dying within them. The pressure from their colleagues, the cafard of schemes run to seed, the cosmic solid weight of the thing....

And me, conceding defeat before I've even darkened the door of this dark inquisition. Forewarned is disarmed and the battle has yet to sound.

"Feeling deliciously sorry for yourself, Kael?"

"You know me too well, Anla petal."

"Bloody wish I did.... Get your pissy little bat off the beam, Shithead."

The skite fell, slotted between two other vehicles. Anla locked the systems with the bleak sound of a terminal file closure.

Kael regarded his place of work. An exemplar of Revived New Paedoarchitectonics: 3991 *(orth. date)*—a good year for insights, that—great vulgar dodecahedrons in silver, copper, gold, sparkling diamondoid, perched on spindly stilts in a sea of leveled lava, temporary mechfab grouprooms with an air of pre-dating human settlement, and all set to outlast time itself. Kael and his friend (now colleague) Anla entered by the staff slide en route for the staff room.

A horde of kids surged past.

"Morning Madame Griffith." "Morning Maam Griffith."

"Good morning, educer!" "Nice day, eh?" "Mornngrff."

"Good morning, Rio. Good morning, En. Good morning, Luigi. Morning, all."

A kid knocked Kael's library. "Sorry, sensei," bundling past.

Staff quarters was a box serving the functions of common room, study and store room. Mugs of some nameless beverage stood etching brown rings on piles of resource crap; gazetted advertisements tried conceptually to brighten the place up. Fly away from the ice to work where it's nice. If I was down on the glaciers that's just what I'd do, mate, if I had the seniority. Happily this is where the machines posted me, near my buddy Anla, with a little nudge from Catsize the data king.

The Emperor stood askew in his holo. In a corner an urn bubbled steam. And my fellow workmates, colleagues and cronies-to-be, boasting of their vacations under alien stars, slurping down ersatz. A hearty man greeting Anla, with a flourish of his educer's library.

"Hello Anla, back for another season on the loop? Must rush, I've got your lot from last year."

Kael found a place and sat down, slightly ill. Anla introduced him to various people, some harassed, some resigned, some efficient, some cynical. They milled around, all of them, they milled. Lights blipped. Noise from the isometrics playground slowly eased. Kael heard someone echoing through a repeater system, a harsh disjointed sound. The staff room eddied and drained. The three or four other virgin educers were led away by their appointed superiors. Tramping feet in the corridor. A voice shouted: "Don't run!" Alone. Kael sat and looked at the job vacancies, and the art work. Adhesion had been lost from a corner of *Jerusalem the Golden*; a minaret curved and went through the wall.

A secretary appeared: "Are you Mr. Ponchard?"

"That's me."

"If you wait here, Mr. Grey will vid you and direct you to your class."

"Good."

Grey eh? The co-ordinator himself. Star treatment. Kael, alone again, studied the display boards; hard bright machine script. Playground duty; Control of Entry Implementation Plan Phase One; Tea credit Arrears. There was a knock on the door.

Silence.

Another knock.

Kael shouted: "Come in."

Silence.

Another knock.

"Come in!"

Silence.

Another knock.

Kael got to his feet and walked to the door. A small boy with earnest black eyes looked up at him.

"Please sensei Mr. Trott wants the nucleotide fractionator, sensei."

"Do you know where it is?"

"In the staff room sensei."

"Yeah, but do you have any idea where?"

"No sensei."

Kael looked at the jumble of lockers, panels, desks, winking lights. Hopeless.

"Well, you'd better help me look for it."

The child shuffled his feet and looked down the corridor.

"Come in, there's no one else here."

"It'll be all right sensei."

"But don't you want the fractionator?"

"I'll come back when there's another educer here sensei."

"Suit yourself."

The small scuttled off down the corridor. Kael closed the door, crossed back over the territorial boundary to the land of us, where *us* means what four years ago was *them*. Some distance you've come, Socrates me old fruit—a good three meters and the width of a door.

His library chimed. He opened the comm circuit. A man he'd never seen in his life looked up at him.

"Ah, you must be Mr. Ponchard."

"Mr. Grey?"

"Somebody has interfered with the staff-room controls of the holo projector. Will you activate it please?"

Oh shit, here we go again. Kael stared about him without much optimism.

"The black panel behind the door, under the lavatory-block monitors."

He located the toggle and activated the internal line. A gray man appeared behind him: gray toga-top and trousers, gray skin, gray hair. Kael's eyes went at once to the color settings. No, nicely balanced. Not a ruth immune, surely, with such a post. Cosmetics, then, a little reversible gene work. For the effect. Wisdom, the sanction of the ages. Bugger me.

"How do you do, sir."

"Welcome to Curringal Inlay Basic. You've met Olp Scrancher, the math comptroller?"

"No, I'm a historian."

"Ah yes, but we are a bit understaffed on the math side of things at the moment. I'm sure you'll manage. Plenty of substantial stochastic math in history eh? Now if you'd like to follow the blue arrow to 3C, I'll introduce you to your charges. We'll pulse a proper time table though to your library after break." He vanished, and the guidance system flashed imperatively. The co-ordinator's voice lingered in the empty air. "And see that the 3C projector is turned on when you get there?"

Charioteers, it's all true. Everything that was ever wailed by stoned novices in noisy parties. Galactic historians educing math, stochasticians dragging out the elements of aesthetics, artists instructing in physics, people with no training at all educing anything that came into their heads. A man might expect to be shifted around a bit during training sessions but this is the real thing, kid.

Kael followed the bright blue arrow through corridors dull with the odors of synthetics distinctive as the frozen tang of cryoparlours. A door slid up. Thirty-five unformed faces;

thirty-five kids dazed with pre-medication. The holo projector came on without any prompting from Kael as the arrow faded.

"Good morning 3C."

"Good morning Sensei Grey."

"This is Sensei Ponchard who is joining Basic today—"

2.

Catsize trod the decaying pedestrian pavement.

All this wrought by the unaided hand of man and beast, just two brief centuries ago. Every founding city a time machine, Jericho to gleaming Utopia. This the midden end of the scale.

Glo-panels swung from their posts like remnants of a public hanging. Old datafax and discarded foils lay in sodden drifts against the fences.

Crazed bastards, will they never learn about nonrenewable resources?

The universe is bulging at the seams, ready to come unstuck. You've sustained your pig's garbage economy for an extra two thousand years, by the grace of God and the Charioteers, but where will you be a century hence?

Rotten habits reinforced in stale immortal minds. Fucked. We're all fucked.

The solid bit of overstated gothic revival that housed Anla and Ben stood back from the grimy common behind a well-integrated lawn bordered by a thin orange line of flamebuds, a firm bulwark of order against the creeping sloth of the neighborhood and the impending crash of the Empire.

The original design for gracious living had suffered rude surgery some decades earlier, front split with clinical precision from back. Forward dwelled a batch of young insurance hustlers, proud cultivators of the flower beds. In the lobotomized rear half lived Anla and Ben, unfashionably married.

From their rearguard windows could be seen a small jungle breached only by a short track, the relatively safe passage (through knee-high grass, rampant whisk, man-eating thorn-glee) to the Cathouse, final outpost of civilization.

Around its crumbling brick walls, built by the first Million on Victoria, alien weeds had total dominion. Here no writ of Empire ran. Above its patched slate roof strange birds looked askance. Once the manual laundry to the original pioneer establishment, it was now the home and castle of Catsize the people's poet.

The poet's narrow bed lay along one wall; a purple chest, on which rested a large force-field-fed urn to fuel the poet with beverages, took up another.

In the place where the copper had once rested Catsize had constructed a makeshift fireplace. Less efficient than the right sort of machine, and so a minor sin, but cozy as all get out.

On the marble draining board stood his ornate library, a data treasury rivaling the City Fathers, listing slightly on the board's gentle slope.

One of the twin zinc tubs had been filled with soil, from which sprouted a number of vigorous seedlings, adding a tasteful touch of greenery to these otherwise austere quarters.

A heavy fall of hard-fax covered most of the horizontal surfaces of the cell, piling up in the corners. For all his thaumaturgic command of machines, the poet liked to seize words in his hands.

Catsize entered his laundry. He entered a Medbank url of terrible puissance, pushed the library aside and sat at the draining board lost in contemplation. A cargo vessel hummed low overhead. The seedlings at his elbow were doing well, the autonomics he'd rigged to feed Anla's molt-feathered scowl while they had been away on Newstralia. had done a good job watering them. Still, it was the wrong time of the year to plant them, and they were getting too big for the sink. He decided to throw most of them away and keep just a couple as indoor pot plants. Catsize turned his attention back to the library, and illegally called a private subroutine.

Physicians' names lined up in a long column on the right

hand of the display, their zips and surgery hours on the left. Kael's fathers were listed; he'd avoid those.

He had purchased the code from a disgruntled junkie who had become accustomed to entering his own prescriptions. The zips had been changed after his arrest and no pharmacy in town would respond to them now, but labor deployment appeared to be more tolerant. There was much to be said for Imperial insistence of departmental independence.

The poet reached down and pulled a foil baggie from under the draining board, rummaged through it, found the list he needed and kicked the foil back again. Thistlethwaite and Crosby: *The Text Book of General Medicine* (London, 1913). He'd inlayed the mnemonics on this in an Earth library—the original kind—over a century ago, hard-copied it here, and cleared it. Its categories would be a mystery to physicians on fifth millennium Victoria.

Catsize flicked through it: chronic sleep inversion, tertiary syphilis (a sort of educational disorder ha ha), peripheral neuropathy. That last sounded good; it sounded bad. The class of endogenous ailments which ruth couldn't touch. It might take years of genetic therapy to cure.

He certified himself as unfit for toil due to congenital emergent peripheral neuropathy, cross-indexed one of the medico's zips, added yesterday's date, pulsed the package through to Medbank and anchored it.

The library printer gave him an authoritative hard reference card. He put it in the right hand shoulder pocket of his flack jacket. He extracted a blood-stained handkerchief from one of the purple drawers and stuffed it up his sleeve.

Taking a bundle of fax from the draining board he retired to his bed to read. He selected a few sheets, folded them, placed them neatly in the left hand shoulder pocket and slipped from the Cathouse on dying feet.

§

Catsize the unemployable entered the offices of the Department of Labor at the gentlemanly hour of zenith and took his place on the bench.

Four others sat ahead of him, two bonded women in purdah and a pair of callow pre-ruth babies. With any luck he'd be out within the hour.

Behind their over-mechanized counter Smeeth and Schafschank dragged themselves through the life-affirming round of their daily tasks. Schafschank was the right hand pocket man, Smeeth the patron of the left. To each his due.

Smeeth was fussing about with a filing program. Getting Smeeth's eye was half the battle; between them they would wangle it so that when Catsize's turn came Schafschank was occupied with someone else. A couple of months ago he'd clumsily got stuck with Schafschank for the first time, a miserable pinched-up centenarian gone sour on life, given to innuendoes about the color of Catsize's hair, the state of his dress.

Catsize had slouched in his pod and regarded Schafschank through rheumy eyes, breath wheezing from his lungs in gasps and snorts, fingers going unsteadily to the right hand pocket. Schafschank had banged the code into his device, and the testimonial of disability lit up to quiver under his nose. Liver fluke. He'd moved back a bit at that one, and coughing into the blood-stained rag hadn't been remotely necessary.

Liver fluke had kept him going for a time, the peripheral thing ought to be good for rather longer, but still there must be a limit to Schafschank's credulity. Better to trust in Smeeth and the left hand path.

A printed clock glowed on the wall. Holos invited Catsize to be a man with a mission. One of these missionaries, arrayed in full battle order, a transduction helmet over his face, gesticulated at him with a virus vector.

The neighboring poster forewent images in favor of a tersely worded declaration that all citizens with the appropriate modulus birth date would be library notified of their induction into Imperial Service. The carrot and the stick.

Schafschank finished interviewing a dull man with a drooping moustache. The fellow left, clutching doubtfully at his handwritten introduction to a prospective employer. Shit, surely they could handle all this rote through the datanet. But no, the psychology of it had no doubt been run out by a thousand hand-crafted memetic bugs.

One of the callow youths was beckoned; he shuffled over and dropped into the pod in front of Schafschank's screen-choked desk. Smeeth summoned the other baby.

Catsize viewed a cartoon on the joys of becoming a plasma-welder. Schafschank's youth slouched back to the bench and sat waiting for his friend. She too now clutched an intro-duction, passport to the socialist dignity of labor. Schafschank gestured to the bonded women who both hurried around to huddle at his confessional.

Smeeth released his baby and addressed Catsize in a friendly professional manner:

"Welcome back, had a good time on Newstralia?"

"Not bad."

"Any luck with work up there?"

"No, there was a couple of good jobs going but it's me age, see, they discriminate against over-experienced people."

"Yes, it must be difficult, I can't imagine why they don't give you a pension. Bad precedent of course. I'll see what we've got," he said in a loud brisk tone, "I'm sure we can fix something up for you."

"Jeez, it'd be real good if you could."

Smeeth busied himself with a phatic scan, tagging an occa-sional file, studying it and flicking on. A flush was rising in his cheeks. He glanced over his shoulder at Schafschank's booth.

The bonded women were confessing their sins to the sour pastor of work. Bow five times to the Emperor's holo and work four hours a day for the rest of eternity at a polymerizing machine.

Smeeth dialed his chair forward, leaning over the desk, switching the displays off. Catsize leaned over from his pod.

The brown fibrous partitions curving up from the sides of Smeeth's desk provided furtive cover.

"Get much written?"

"A few good poems."

"Got one with you?"

The left hand pocket. Catsize murmured, hardly needing to glance at the fax in his hands, the words of truth, beauty, turmoil and resignation that Smeeth so longed to hear.

"It's the Nightingsnail Canto, see, got the idea on Newstralia. Here's how it goes:

> Ah, sheet, beast, you hear me? I'm blocked. My skin's tight, hands and feet flying somewhere else: dissociated, Nightingsnail, stonkered on the toxic narcotic of projective empathy. You're okay, that's no hassle. I'm ripped by your singing, man. Lucky sod, symbiotic with your green shadowy beeches, singing it up about summer, no repressions. Actually I could do with a glass of Old Earth wine, snail, some vintage that's been lying a long time in a cool cellar, with its tangs of grape, green country vines, French peasants at dance and song, sunburnt bastards hooting and falling about in some fucking drunken fertility riot. A cold glass from the warm fields, instinct with true, delicate inspiration, with beaded bubbles winking at the brim, claret-purple at the mouth. I'd knock it back, snail, and be right up there with you in the night forest.

Smeeth was breathing. "Listen, that what was it 'wine', can you get that on Victoria?"

Catsize regarded him mysteriously. "Mate of mine was picking grapes up in the tropics a few years back, I reckon the vintage'd be just right now."

"I shall order a liter. I'm sorry, go on, it's marvelous."

"Okay." Catsize read in his louche, graveled voice:

§

Yeah, I'd let it all go, piss off the mind-fucks you fine shell-wings never heard of, all the weary, feverish, fretful crap that's bringing us down. In the final analysis all we can do is sit round listening to each other's groaning: the poor old buggers in their twitching, endless boredom, the kids with borrowed memories in their bones, facing forever. Brains? Nothing there but grief and despair. Beauty? The babes' wet eyes soon dull over, and their puppyfat heartaches turn to vapid bitching two days after they've declared their love.

Ah crap, I'm just feeling sorry for myself. I don't need booze or buzz to get the snail-trip on. My brain might be knackered, but the old lyric rave always turns the trick. Ahem:

The night's sweet and warm; somewhere up there, in a cluster of stars, there's a foddle moon, though you'd never know if it weren't for the odd breeze pushing aside the dark heavy leaves that hang down over the mossy winding footpaths.

There are flowers underfoot, and a soft incense of blossom from the boughs, but it's too dim to see anything much. I can identify them fairly well by their scents, though, the air's so still: all the summer flora: grass, thickets, wild fruit-trees, white hawthorns, those succulent briars you find out in the pastures, fast fading violets covered up in leaves; and the earliest of the summer flowers, musk-rose blossoms, full of dewy wine, where the humming bees hover on summer evenings—"

Blinking damp eyes, Smeeth interrupted with an apologetic cough. "Um, I hope you'll forgive me if I mention that to the best of my knowledge the flora and fauna you itemize are not known on Newstralia, I think. I've made a minor study of—"

"No, it's Old Earth ecology," Catsize said with some irritation. "Poetic license, mate."

"Oh. Yes I see that now. Please continue."

"'On nights like that'," Catsize read,

> I stand there listening to the murmuring insects, often enough half persuaded of the virtues of death, quite relaxed, rather wishing my lungs would pack it in. I've got that number heavy on me now. No offense, snail, but hearing your ecstatic rave, death seems, well, attractive. A painless death at midnight. On you'd sing, to my dead deaf ears. Getting into death, with your plainchant for my requiem.
>
> But there's nothing about death or ruth in your DNA program, is there? Snail, you're just the momentary cross-section of an endless cloned continuum. No awareness of brutalized generations to bring you down, sport. Exactly the same voice I'm hearing now was heard millennia ago by the Charioteers; it's a stamped-in piece of phylogeny.

The furtive words spun their web of joy, sorrow, life and forgotten death while Smeeth fiddled blindly with his scanning system. Catsize finished his tolling fugue and sat back, a lotus conspirator. Smeeth looked dazed.

"Well, I'm sorry, there doesn't seem to be anything on file really suitable for you, perhaps something will turn up next week."

"Oh, jeez, righto then, see youse later."

Catsize slunk out of the offices of the Department of Labor, unemployed, unemployable, the unwilling recipient of the Empire's credit. He sloped through the business quarter, revived slightly at the sight of a pub, walked briskly across the lawn and entered the fuggy dark of the saloon. He ran his finger down the list of available comestibles, pressed his order, and shot a light buzz. A professional working poet taking luncheon at his club.

3.

Voices came indistinctly up from the lawn: Catsize expounding, Jard laughing, Anla dry and ironic—words without, hum of insects loitering on the margins of the screen, crackle of roasting protein in the kitchen. Theri heard Sofy open the oven door and add something from the garden, rich odors entering the air, smothered as the door clicked shut.

She walked around the room picking up symphonic crystals, putting them back.

The peace she should have felt evaded her. The setting was at least as conducive to peace as usual: this good room, the late autumn day, Jard and his guests drinking Catsize's whimsical wine under the genecopied trees, the prospect of three days away from that bloody apt she shared with Kael. By rights, it all should have induced a relaxed good humor.

The back of Jard's old house fitted into a ledge cut in the hillside. Here at the front it tottered out into space on a line of crumbling concrete pillars.

Wattle engulfed most of the durobond walls and a continuous silt of gum leaves and twigs clogged the run-offs. At night the native grundles scratched in the roof and pissed on the ceiling, discoloring the plastic.

Jard made an occasional effort to deter the beasts with pheromones, but his fortifications degraded after a week at best. Anla said he was secretly fond of the grundles and would be upset if they didn't regain dominion after a token exile.

The living room was long, low, untidy. A random selection of prints, hand-wrought paintings, engravings and maps—not a holo, in sight—covered most of the wall area that wasn't plants. It stood for Theri as antithesis to the anonymous pale apt she had left that morning, bowling up over the urban sprawl in Catsize's skite. God, what a disgusting, soulless place.

She thought of the apt with suppressed rage: bloody little box, stacked with the other little boxes for existing in. All that is necessary to sustain life, provided by the Empire's minions. *Conapt.: f-furn.: lib.: bd.rm.: dn.rm.: kitch.: dp.sp.: no pregs.* The table we eat from, the chairs we sit in, the library we commune with, the bed we sleep in, the bed we make love in, the squeak it contrives to make, duplicated in every other cheap, mechfab box of tricks in the condominium, right down to the bloody technically impossible squeak, no doubt.

Nine identical squeaks from nine identical beds neatly arranged in a pre-stressed plast frame. Three by three; not less than nine and rarely more than thirty people-units, iron filings in the stochastic field, squeaking out their miserable lusts when the day's toil is done and the night's begun:

squeaksqueaksqueak

squeaksqueaksqueak

squeaksqueaksqueak

She walked to the view wall. Under the trees Jard was bouncing the baby on his knee. Alleles shuffled courtesy of Mother Nature, none of your mechfab clone rubbish there, mate, a one-off special.

Catsize, Anla and the star-hopper woman, who was apparently in more or less permanent residence at the moment, lay around in the middle of a small collection of wine flasks. Jeanine, that's right; funny name. Came from some galactic cluster to hell and gone out of this sector. Probably over a thousand years old, restless with wanderlust.

Kael and Ben were nowhere in sight. Theri presumed they had gone for a walk.

Bloody hope it does him some good—all those animals and birds running around the bush doing their animal things, might give him a clue, be good for the gonads, get his mind off that bloody Basic Inlay crap. Maybe he'll screw me better out here, maybe being the second squeak in the top row is secretly sapping his virility.

Would he like to lay the star-hopper? She certainly looks as if she could do with some herself. Does lust go with wanderlust? Doesn't seem to say much, just pouts around the place looking sexy in a sluttish sort of way. Wonder how many kids she's had? Scores, probably. Would Kael be interested?

For an instant, a sickening image entered Theri's mind, iconography from her parents' Christer Revival shrine: the moist, bovine eyes, the slimy, pulsing heart held out like a bait in the pierced hand.

Theri shuddered. If Jeanine could bring out half a gram of aggression in old gentle Jesus down there she'd be doing society a favor.

Jard looked up and waved to her. Theri waved back, but remained in the room, calling a Databank thing he'd recommended. She heard Jard bring the infant in to be spruced up by the tending autonomics.

He came silently to where she sat, gave her a glass of the grape stuff and, leaning over her shoulder, read the title of her program: Hector's *Equestrian Journal*. He quoted some of it verbatim, resting a hand gently on her bare shoulder as he spoke, the stanzas flowing with a rich, familiar cadence. Placing the half empty flask by the chair, he went down again to the group under the trees.

What would Jard be like in bed? An improvement on old Am-I-hurting-you.

Chariots almighty, all I was doing was moaning a bit and he has to stop in mid-fuck and enquire about the state of my health. "Am I hurting you?" If only he bloody had of been.

If I said "Stop!" to that nut two seconds before his orgasm he'd pull up short and ask with infinite concern what the matter was.

And if I said I'd decided I was no longer in the mood for sex, would he curse me? Would he hit me? Would he hell, he'd just stroke the hair from my eyes and tell me in a voice squirming with compassion and love that he quite understood and maybe I'd feel better in the morning. Kael's warm and loving, but he's feeble, poor shit, nice but feeble.

Jard with his silly flight-from-Trantor mystique and heroic universe (Good and Evil, Authority and Autonomy, locked in mortal combat, giving symbolic values to quite ordinary events) would not be feeble. She envied Sofy the year to be spent with Jard in Isaacville on Trantor—a better bet than hanging around bloody Bolte with Kael.

§

The group dispersed. Kael decided to stay with Sofy to clear away the lunch, while the others drifted up the hill. Ben had suggested that the tree cut down three years ago ought, in fact, as planned, be made into a bridge. Jard had acknowledged that the wood was probably well enough seasoned by now.

Kael incinerated the plates, handing the cutlery to Sofy. Tussey, truant from her tending machine, played under foot, naked and brown. Kael launched an inquisition about the baby: how much did she weigh at birth, when would she start to walk, did Sofy favor early booster inlays, how many times a day did she need to be fed?

The child in question started to grizzle, and Kael picked her up. This started her crying in earnest. Twisting in Kael's arms, she leaned toward Sofy; he relinquished her.

Sofy went out to the verandah, sat in one of the floaters, depolarized her shirt and maternity uplift. The baby gave a final wail and fastened hungrily onto the proffered nipple. Kael sat on the verandah floor, his back against a strut, watching the child sucking blindly at her mother's milkheavy breasts.

If Kael's three homosexual fathers had been present, they'd have turned away in delicate disgust; they regularly denounced this atavistic practice, adducing the purest value-free medical evidence.

Who knew what heinous infections Sofy might be carrying? Without ruth, the baby was in appalling danger.

She looked healthy enough. Miniature fingers clutched at the soft flesh, the crooked ridge of a vein moving elastically under the insistent massage.

Sofy smiled at her sucking child and winced slightly, transferring the clutching hand from her breast to her middle finger.

"Her nails are too long, they're like little blades."

Kael covered his eyes with his right arm and felt under the palm of his left hand the rough wood of the verandah floor.

Afternoon noises blended with Sofy's humming. An occasional bird sounded from somewhere near the creek. The baby gurgled.

The air was thick with the scent of eucalyptus and the heavy, sticky smell of Sofy's milk. Kael pressed his forearm more tightly across his eyes and watched the whirling spots of light changing from red to a radioactive indigo. Like insights erupting from inlayed peptide chains.

Voices punctuated by the hiss and pop of wood-trimming came from the hill above the dwelling. Sofy's bare feet came down onto the floor. Tussey's weight descended to his chest.

Kael took his arm away from his face and held the swaying infant with both hands. Crouched beside him, Sofy closed her garment.

"Play with her till she burps, then she can go back to the tender."

Kael glanced from the now smiling infant to her mother. Sofy was a big, quiet woman; like Anla, he realized, on the rare occasions when Anla wasn't throwing her weight around and telling everyone what to do—a sort of relaxed, maternal Anla.

He wondered what kind of mother Anla would make and decided she would be terrible, for the first century at any rate, giving her children strict instructions to obey no one, conscripting them to the ranks of the libertarians.

Tussey laughed at the faces he pulled and burped a frothy glob of milk onto his chest.

Together, they put the infant into her autonomic cocoon, waited a few minutes above the darkened bubble until she was properly asleep, and walked up the hill to join the tree trimmers.

"Put that damned marvel of science aside, there's only one authentic way to trim a log."

Amazing Catsize came bounding into the clearing waving a formidable slab of edged steel from which jutted a smooth, slightly curved length of wood. Charioteers, Anla thought, it's a frontiersman's axe. He handed it to Jard with an ironic bow. Prerogative of the host to maim himself first.

"It's wonderful, Catsize. Where did you get it?"

"They haven't all been recycled, you know. Planet used to be littered with them. You can clear a world with defoliant bugs, but the first Million's got to have something to work with before they get their technology to the electronic stage. No, you dolt, treat it cybernetically: gravity provides the energy, you only use your muscles to guide the stroke."

Anla sat against a tree watching her clone swinging the axe. So now he's off to pacified Trantor for a Sabbatical with Sofy-kitten and my new hemi-sister.

Back to where, bright young man from the Dominions up at the regional datasink, he met my X-donor. Got off with the daughter of an Autonomist lawyer. Took her up the river on summer evenings in punts.

Some feat in those days—hard enough to contract a liaison at all, what with all the pre-action paranoia of the place. Off for an ambiguous lay in the flat fields outside Isaacville gold and brown with the corn and swallows in the twilight and brown cigars in little smoky pubs.

Very Old New York. And is summer still a golden sea? and so on and so forth. Standing in the back of the punt in massive turned-up boots and open fronted blouse like every other budding eighties poet.

Sensitive fresh-eyed baby with his colonial strine accent rapidly submerging under a dry Trantor twang. Did he really know what was going on? How well did he understand his lawyer's daughter as she lay in the bottom of those punts in her plain virginal dresses, kicking off her clodhoppery sandals and trailing her long white feet in the water?

Clumsy bloody barges, shoveled along with those great phallic poles. They took great pride in their style, shoving the pole in the water, heaving away. It's all a matter of balance and rhythm, he once told me—quite seriously.

Was he really screwing her then, in those fields or in the furtive beds of his pure college? They prided themselves equally on their purity and their puns, that lot, if reports are to be believed. Little wonder they couldn't raise an effective army.

It's unlikely that he got his end in, then. Surely if he had he would have brought her away to the Dominions while there was still time. Or did the psychology of the thing work the other way?

Anyway, she was a sturdy anarchist, would have boxed his ears.

So he went underground with them like some knight errant, exchanging his barge-pole for a neutron rifle left over from the last action.

Then it was finished; they were out-programmed by the Empire's memetic bugs, and she refused to leave when the visiting colonials were Millioned. Gave him an X-chromosome to remember her by.

Tearful remonstrations, no doubt, but he had me grown before he left. I'm the living intersection of banality and sensitive courage. And now he's going back with his new lady and his new baby: off to regain the innocence of youth, it'd make a good short poem, old revo coming home to the world of his dreams.

"Hey Theri, I've thought of a good poem."

"What about?"

"Well, there's this academic who'd seduced his first girl on a punt near Isaacville, and two hundred years later he goes back to the place with another girl. They take a punt on the river, but he's misread the rain schedule and the poor bugger can't manage the pole properly and the boat keeps running into the bank. He gets the pole tangled up in thick weeds.

"The rain get worse and the girl gets soaked and the man falls into the river and the whole thing is a total disaster. So they eventually get the boat back to the landing stage, by which time the girl is furious and the bloke is moody and depressed. So he takes her to a pub he used to know.

"He thinks it will be warm and old with a roaring log fire and full of baby graduates arguing about the road to autonomy, but it's been tarted up and due to forestry restrictions the open fire has been replaced by a muse randomizer and it's full of purple-haired yobos talking about zam.

"So the man buys two cigars and gives one to the girl who refuses to light it and demands a buzz. So the old boy smokes both of the nasty things himself and the girl starts to flirt with one of the horrid yobos, has a quarrel with the academic and leaves in the yobo's skite.

"So he starts buzzing and by the time the pub closes he's good and blasted. He decides to walk to Isaacville, because that's what they used to do when he was a baby—climb out of their purity cells and walk to Isaacville through the strange shadows of the moons and stare up reverently at the famous claustropod where the Sensei was hammering away unceasingly at his library.

"But the trouble is, there are all sorts of new multilevels, and the commons have been changed, and he loses his way. He can't find the hitching bleep code on his library so he staggers about half the night and ends up heading towards the local Teleport."

Theri was smiling like a loon, egging her on with eager little grunts and nods. Some of the others had drifted up and stood listening, smirking or puzzled, depending on how well they know her.

"He finds a transport autocafe and collapses into a seat and orders coffee. He sits there brooding until a freighter pilot asks him where he's going. He says he wants to get back to Isaacville, so the trucky gives him a lift. And because he looks so done-in the trucky give him a couple of adrenergics to shoot. By the time he gets back to Isaacville he's quite fast.

"And as he walks among the deserted buildings it seems to him that Isaacville is filled with the companions of his youth. Codswallop and good old Sprogget appear walking arm in arm across a cobbled common. His old tutors and professors go creaking past on ancient frontier bicycles. And there's his dear friend Snod with his cigar in one hand and his library in the other. But as he rushes up to speak to them they disappear.

"And then suddenly the clouds break and the moons come beaming down in great multihued shafts of light and the front of his old college shines before him, all ghostly and timeless. And he knows what he must do.

"He runs toward the college and clambers through the monitors and starts to climb the face of the computer complex. He climbs like a man possessed, which he is.

"At times it seems to him that he's not alone on the face, but on a climbing rope with Sprogget and Codswallop. At one stage he comes to an impasse, but he knows what to do, he reaches up and finds the gleaming plastic piton that he and Sprogget hammered in all those centuries ago, and with a great effort he pulls himself over the impasse and climbs on.

"His drugged heart is pumping away fit to burst, nothing ruth can do to combat biochemical self-abuse, and he's gasping for breath but he's so delirious he doesn't feel it.

"Finally he get to the top of a spire and stands there hanging onto the ionizing nipple and the moons blazing out again and all Isaacville is spread below him, city of scholarly detachment, ornate and enchanted. He knows he has come back where he belongs and a great peace floods over him.

"Then an Imperial militia skite hoves alongside and plucks him off, threatening to charge him with seditious trespass. But after one look into his old, tame eyes they release him with a warning, and he remembers that he forgot to turn the infant's tender on and the kid'll be all covered in poo from head to toe, and he gets out quietly and trudges home."

Anla took a drink of wine and grinned back at Theri.

§

Hot with confusion and guilty mirth, Theri looked at Jard still hacking at the tree. His youth's face was red with exertion and lined with sweat, his dashiki flapping. She watched him take a last swing at the contused branch; he passed the barbaric implement to Ben, who took over the amputation. Probably he hadn't heard a thing.

Jard sat down on a log vacated by Ben and drank a glass of wine in one mouthful. Some of it went up his nose. The sweat had dampened his abundant hair, which lay on his scalp in a thick black mat. Theri stood up and went for a walk.

§

Squatting on his heel carving a stick with his knife, Catsize watched Anla watching Theri. He wondered how valid Anla's perception really was. She had only spoken to him with complete candor two or three times since he had known her. Normally they maintained a dry, sparring relationship, continually maneuvering for position without engagement.

Now she joined him as he tried, with little success, to turn a piece of fibrous native wood into a figure of a horse. Anla sat on the ground.

"It's like a bloody levee-en-masse poem."

Catsize raised the roughly shaped bit of wood in his hand and, regarding it, nodded. "That was the main thrust of my artistic intention. A touch more off at the pointed end and I imagine that even a purist will readily mistake it for the Imperial Conclave in High Session."

"All these people, Catsize."

"They just look like a bunch of Victorian yobos cutting up a tree to me."

"Listen, fuckface, what we have here is a small group of interrelated people milling about in a sexual force-field."

"Sexual force-field? How uncouth."

"Catsize, stop being deliberately thick, you know as well as I do. Theri and Jard are attracted to each other. Kael and Sofy are all over each other with that little bundle. Ben would like to lay Jeanine and Jeanine would lay any one of us."

"And you think this is going to happen?"

"No, nothing is going to happen. Unless you make it."

He recoiled theatrically. "What madness is this?"

"Look, you're always getting people to do things. The first bloody time we met you, you got Ben and Kael to kneel down on the common in the middle of Bolte. People are always getting caught up in your little psychodramas; the moment you walk into a room people start reacting to you—you can tell by the way they start talking, the phrases they use. And you know as well as I do why they do it. People want to act out their fantasies and you provide the means, you turn life into a scenario and let the script take over the people. Everyone expects it of you, it's your style, it's what you do in your composition and your mode of living. It would be so easy for you. I wouldn't mind betting Theri is secretly hoping you will anyway. Everyone is half-smashed as it is, they don't know how to handle wine, which you must have known when you brought it up here. By tonight they'll be supersaturated. And you're the crystal."

Catsize's knife slipped and sliced the embryo tail from his horse. He threw the chip of wood away.

"I can't remember *your* ever getting taken over by a character role, Anla."

"Maybe that's because I'd rather live life straight without repressing all my desires."

"You've vid too many poems."

"I haven't vid half the poems you have. That you've written, probably."

"Well, what the hell do you expect me to do with this little levee? Get them all to pretend to be the inmates of a frontier bawdy house or something?"

"Something like that. More subtle I imagine."

"Why?"

"It'd be good for them."

"You rather fancy yourself as the Charioteer, don't you? The dark lady brooding unseen over her subjects, the omnipotent chess player with her human pieces."

"Look, don't come the analytic program with me, Catsize, you might be Theri's confessor, you're not mine."

"And what about you, Anla, what's going to be your place in this proposed bawdy house? What are you going to be doing while Ben is screwing Jeanine?"

"That's up to you, you're master of ceremonies."

"But my dear Anla, it has hardly escaped my attention that in the elementary paired scheme of things you've provided, the only couple left unaccounted for is you and me."

She looked demurely at the leaf-strewn ground.

"Anla, look at me."

Anla held Catsize's gaze, neither laughing nor serious, neither superior nor subject. After half a minute Catsize put an end to the contest. "And this is to be my fee for providing you with your bawdy house, the body and soul of Madam Anla Elsbeth Griffith for the space of one night?"

"Catsize, I can't wait."

"You won't have to, I'm not going to do it."

Anla remained silent for a minute. She stood up, then, and bent over Catsize, kissing him quickly on his mouth, and walked at once to the tree. She relieved Ben of the axe and started to cut at the branches with sure, easy strokes, in marked contrast to the way her husband had been slogging at the battered limbs.

Catsize watched her for a while, then went in search of Theri, whom he found sitting by the side of the creek, ineffectually throwing rocks at the brackish water.

PART FIVE

1.

The inquisitorial element was holing up in the lounge bar. Kael duly lounged in a plast web spun out from untenably frail tetrahedral supports, and looked with distaste at the vigor-giving mash lumped on his plate.

Insidious melodiazam oozed from a ubiquitous point-source mosaic into his ears. The chatter from those of the staff already present stifled his thoughts. The prospect of a whole afternoon given over to a marathon staff moot filled him with frustrated gloom. It was an event one could not afford to sleep through; nor could you conceivably manage to pay attention for more than half a minute at a time.

Kael felt his buzz ebb and made his way to the bar for another. The least a man could do, he decided, get pleasantly scorched.

He brought the buzz back to the curried mash; Olp Scrancher had arrived and settled heavily into the opposite web.

A professional, Scrancher, an old hand at the game. Liked by the kids—those who'd developed a taste for sarcasm anyway. Liked by the staff—those who wanted a nice smooth progression through the educing ritual, which was all of them.

Well, I like you too, Olp, you're a good bloke under all that time-wearied cynicism, but you're not getting me with your traditional certainties.

"How are you finding educing?"

"All right."

"Not like you thought it would be?"

Kael shrugged. "Not much different."

"Funny thing—when I first met you I thought, 'Hello, here's one of those weirdies that believes in letting the kids do what they want, random data play and fondling each other's genitals in the isometrics room.'"

"You thought that?"

"We do get them, you know."

"I suppose it takes all sorts to make a world."

"You're dead right there, Kael my boyo, but why they should all go educing I don't know. The coding error bucket, I suppose, nowhere else for them."

"What happens to them?"

"Either come to their senses or go mad. Stark staring bonkers. Strip them down for enzymes."

Scrancher wolfed his mash and lumbered off to the tea dispenser. Kael contemplated the pattern crawling across the mauve carpet.

He leaned confidentially over his steaming mug of tea to the subsiding Scrancher: "Tell you what, Olp, I did have a few screwy ideas about pedagogy."

"See, what did I tell you?"

"Yeah, I thought all you had to do was treat kids as if they were human beings and the little buggers would behave like human beings."

"Some hope."

"I thought if you got them interested in the substance of their inlays they'd set their own problems and find the answers just popping into their heads, and there'd be no need to keep levering it out."

"Dangerous paradigm, Kael old son, you were confusing them with mature adults. Half our job is to stop them pulling the wrong data out of latent memory and running riot."

"Yeah, but Olp I was into autonomous evocation, that sort of thing precisely. I genuinely felt that if you let the little dears run their own affairs, and form their own hypotheses on the basis of their life-experiences, and test them against the data from their inlays and in the labs over here, there'd be no need to medicate them and keeping on shouting all the time."

"The iron fist in the velvet glove, Kael, it's the only way."

Kael leaned closer, confidential. "It only took me a couple of weeks of shop floor experience to show me that I was absolutely right."

Scrancher reacted sluggishly, studying Kael's deadpan face. "Come again?"

"It was dead right, Olp, everything I ever thought."

Scrancher laughed, a friendly shared-joke laugh, but Kael caught the edge of nervousness, the momentary suspicion of a flaw in the armor.

"Charioteers, Kael, I thought you were serious for a minute."

Kael laughed guilelessly.

"You'd believe anything, Olp."

Anla and the twitchy aesthetician arrived. The conversation turned to the rising incidence of pair marriages.

§

If inertia is indeed equivalent to gravitational mass, Anla thought apathetically, and time in the vicinity of a great enough mass is dilated, stretched out, slowed down, this would help to explain my ennui.

The staff moot dragged on, time winding down by the minute. The heating system was in an overproductive phase and the radiator near Anla announced its presence with the verve of a small but feisty star.

This was the biggest room in the complex and hence appropriated for such occasions. The desks were childsize, too low for the forty-odd adults they now accommodated, but the inbuilt libraries were handy, permitting the sly exchange of witticisms by other than vocal means. Humor is nothing more than the continuation of war by other means. Syntactic-semantic loops, old seesaws.

Anla looked around the open corral of desks: what's meant to be achieved by the whole jamboree? Lethargy pandemic. Kael over there looking attentive; clever the way he's picked that up, taking in even less than I am, probably. Scrancher getting ready to say something. Cold insects outside droning to their deaths in the window screen, much the same noise as the gray man. Would have been good to stay in the pub with Kael; buzzed too much as it is, almost asleep.

Anla dozed off at the back of the room, woke with a start and tried listening to the gray words

"...seems to be a final year group who are the main offenders and at their age they can only set a bad example to the younger children...."

Wish I was still at tertiary like Theri, drinking coffee at leisure, arguing with her tutors, firing away at her library, while we're stuck here listening to this bullshit.

Poor old Kael, he's started to fidget, he's even less cut out for this work thing than I am. Doing this for a thousand years. The mind cringes. Let's all follow in Catsize's gypsy path.

Out the window she could see a couple of small girls from 2B walking across a common, a sight to put our co-ordinator's blood pressure at risk: holding hands and talking non-stop, gladly forsaking an afternoon's noetic dredging so that this important meeting could be held.

Anla punched through a message to Kael's desktop: *And the dead are many.* Kael looked up and smiled; her screen danced to his fingers: *According to leading authorities there's only one moldering in the soil for every quadrillion still on the go, even if you count in all the police actions. A Friend.*

Anla punched for the time: 1525. We must have a tea-break soon, even old grayness needs oiling occasionally. The brew that cheers but does not inebriate—pity.

A slight change in position from the more attentive of our crew; must be something that directly affects us. It might be a merry jape to invert the color values on his holo-projector.

"...so it will be necessary for the rolls to be updated after calisthenics as well as before leaving the grounds, which means that the staff taking isometrics will have to blah blah know that this means more work for those concerned blah blah blah blah the only way...."

So that's what it's all about, those kids from Karry's group pissing off early and spending the afternoon in the open-market autocafes playing the starwar machines, in preference to building vim and grit. A commendable value judgement, used to do the same class of thing myself, zinging off with my muse.

A voice: "But maybe the kids are occupying themselves better in the cafes."

General laughter, increasing noticeably as Grey joins in, the solid phantom, giving his seal of approval to the jest. Has anyone ever seen the man in the flesh? Perhaps he's just a computer simulation, the rule-book leavened by gracious optional subroutines.

"Education in the school of life, eh Mr. Ponchard? Do you think we could make it a semester credit? I'm sure the proprietors would award diplomas."

More laughter. Nothing like a bit of repartee to liven up a moot. With evident anger Kael settled back into his cramped chair. Does he think my laughter a betrayal? She saw him sit forward again to spell it out:

"If we're going to provide a learning situation in which the kids are able to get some experience in making decisions that actually affect their lives, instead of just coughing up data and canned conclusions from their peptide inlays, then maybe we *ought* to allow them to choose between playing phiz-ed games and playing strategy machines."

Anla felt a spasm of genuine alarm. For a moment it seemed that he would start proselytizing for free cognitive exploration. There's a time and a place, Kael.

Only a few smiles. Grey moving in quickly; enough of this nonsense. "They are meant to be at calisthenics and they are deliberately breaking an explicit rule; we cannot be seen even tacitly to condone that."

"Then maybe it shouldn't be a rule."

"It's a Department Regulation, enforced throughout the Empire."

Kael collapsed back. Sorry kiddo, no possible answer to that. You'll learn, as I did.

"And now I think it's time for tea."

§

Kael, depressed and tired, sipped his beverage. Anla over there in her red knitted dress; something worth looking at anyway. Did she really think I was joking, at first, or just that my little statement of policy was tactically ill-advised? A fine wench, Anla. What would she really be like in bed? If she ever leaves Ben properly I suppose I'll find out. Oh, the stupid, stupid shits.

2.

Ben and Catsize strode through the supply district, Ben swinging a foil-filled bag, Catsize expounding, gesticulating, a new satire forming in his fevered brain, a new outrage. Abruptly the poet turned gray and dropped to a slouch, his torso hanging like a sack. Ben stared in horrified alarm. From his sagging mouth, Catsize said, "Just seen the man from the labor exchange, he thinks I've got peripheral neuropathy."

"He thinks you've got what?'

"I bugged their core. It's impossible for me to work, due to my endogenous peripheral neuropathy."

"Shit, mate, how long do they give you to live?"

"Not long if that bugger Schafschank sees me jumping around on the common."

"But I thought they employed you as a poet?"

"Not this month, they haven't. I'm a central emergent genetic malfunction this month."

"Versatile little fellow, aren't you?"

Catsize and Ben slipping into a store. The sick man revived sharply, running and jumping between appetizing holos, dodging the honest shoppers. "As I was saying, this provocative little piece is based on that ludicrous assertion advanced by some pundit in the Imperial Musicology Division when everything was bellyaching about the propriety and decadence of training sperm whales to sing Gregorian chant at a hundred fathoms. While you've got your arm extended I'd rather fancy some scowl eggs."

"The yard is littered with scowl eggs."

"No, it's not, Anla's beast is bloody roosting again. Well, I won't go into it all now, it was a cretinous argument and the pundit got pummeled a bit by other windy bladders and the whales kept on wailing and it's obvious from your attentive face that you've never heard of this important contribution to our on-going transgalactic culture."

"It's not so much that," Ben said. "What are whales?"

"Ah shit. Adrift in the data entropy vortex again. Well, all that's by way of background, anyway, and I'm not sure yet how I'll get it across, but I've no doubt it'll be full of poignant pathos and aggravating hubris and the bittersweet pang of success and failure in a flawed universe. So, this—"

A girl with ancient, demented eyes and a wicker basket caught his arm.

"My dear?" Catsize was gallant.

"Excuse me, young man, you remind me of my father."

"Eh?"

"Yes, he's Old King Cole."

"Not the merry old soul?"

"Yes, that's right, he's a secret libertarian agent and every time he goes to Chomsky he comes back with a beard."

"Good grief."

"Yes, especially in winter."

They had halted before an elevator shaft. The doors opened. Ben guided the dazed, pinkcheeked, pretty old woman into the elevator. Oddly, there was some resemblance to Catsize.

"Well, goodbye father, it's been nice talking to you." The doors closed.

Ben and Catsize looked at one another and ran home, lobbing a carton of scowl eggs back and forth between them.

3.

"Shit, it's cold."

The swirling water called for a quick impromptu dance. Toes chilled, gasping, they made for higher ground, establishing a camp in a seaward hollow of the dunes.

Ben cut the skite out of the cybernet and dropped toward the coast. The sea appeared through thinning wisps, mottled by the winter sunlight. The gray angle of the horizon cleanly undercut the confused jumble of clouds and pale sky.

Low walls of sad scrub hedged the sunken dropspace, combed to a scruffy conformity by the prevailing winds. Only one other vehicle stood in the area, a scarlet sportskite with a decorative skeleton jigging in futile vulgarity.

Ben and Theri ran up the slope to the deserted beach, jumping, arms outstretched, in the wind, slithering to a spread-eagle on the loose sand. A strong, insistent surf was breaking, glass-green and hollow, the spray driven back in slow, high, tearing sheets.

Kael and Anla followed with the support equipment: a couple of filament blankets and a heavy foil of food. By the water's edge the sand was cold and hard. A powerful arctic wave, migrating to the equator for the season, hissed up the beach, soaking bare feet, catching the hem of Anla's black velvet cloak.

Anla sat in the redoubt and looked at the sea. Above the horizon the silver pinpoint of a freighter danced. Rather closer to shore, but beyond the farthest line of breakers, the black stick-figure of a body-skier skimmed on his jets. He turned for the beach, hovering amid spray, propitiating the heaving water.

The ocean brought him slowly landward, ahead of a swelling wave. The skier flattened, his laminar field extending to form a lifting body. The wave reached him, angled his torso to its steepening front. He caught the swell, continuously falling along the uprising face of the wave.

The skier seemed now to be riding smoothly on his feet, standing poised and languid, effortlessly shearing away to his right, cutting a long, sloping swath through the gray-green water.

A crest of shattering crystals, the top of the wave started to disintegrate in the wind, white and fragmented. The structure of the wave broke in two places, before and behind the racing skier, the hollow water folding slowly over upon itself, trapping a tunnel of air which exploded in the aftermath of foam, throwing up plumes of spray. On his unbroken section of the wave the skier continued to slide to the right, hounded from behind by the curling break, rushing like a lemming toward the other flank of confusion.

Half a second before engulfment he shifted his center of mass, flicked his torso round to speed toward the other break. The gap in the double avalanche narrowed mind-wrenchingly; the skier turned again, trapped. The two breaks met in a tempest of foam.

Under for a second, lost in the freezing melee, the skier emerged almost instantly, his extended field visible in the white confusion. Head first, he cleared the wave, shuddering slightly on the flat surface of its forerunner. Like a black projectile he shot straight towards the shore.

The wave diminished, crossed a deeper channel, mutated into a bonsai version of its former magnificence, broke again and rushed forward for its final fling up the beach.

With bravura insolence the skier came to his feet again, the jet gusting at his back.

Twenty meters from the abrasive sand he flipped through 180 degrees, deserting the wave, dropped to his belly and started to skim with delphinian ease toward renewed battle with the incoming surf, making for the quietness beyond the first line of breakers, preparing for the next run.

Theri turned from the spectacle and rolled herself in a filament, starting to vid the ageless sonnets:

They that have power to hurt, and will do none,
That do not do the thing they most do show

Kael and Ben left for a walk along the empty beach, searching for edible shellfish, a more acceptable solecism than roast foddle flesh. Only Anla sat, hunched in her cloak, watching the lonely body-skier pressing ahead with humanity's immemorial struggle against the elements.

§

Theri looked up from the sonnets. Anla, some brooding bird of prey, continued to watch the skier, who was now plodding across the white sand. His jet rig was nowhere in sight, presumably already locked in the tasteless sportskite.

The black heat-suit that covered his torso had a groin flap sealed at his pelvis, no doubt for greater ease of whipping it out and whipping it back in again. Theri stifled a snort; it bore a strong resemblance to the romper suits recommended for incontinent infants.

She watched the man laboring up the slanting sand to their hollow. His face still held traces of summer tan. Theri reactivated the sonnets, flicking them to auditory. An actor's fruity tones came softly from her library, a barely comprehensible rendition of the original phonemic values.

She silently mouthed the inevitable request to herself: You women wouldn't have a spare buzz by any chance?

"Hello, I couldn't bot a hit from you two, could I? I must have left my stash at home, I've been dying for a buzz all day."

Theri turned the sound up slightly. "You don't look too dead to me. Don't Skyhogs have dispensers on the panel?"

"It's seized up.... To tell you the truth I've had nothing but trouble from that crate ever since I got it. I'm crediting it on a new Zinger next week." He squatted in the sand beside them.

"Good for you, I hope the new dispenser's well stocked."

Theri returned to her poems. Anla silently produced an intoxicant from the food foil and offered it to the skier. She shot one herself, while Theri grunted a gruff refusal, keeping her filament-warmed back to the man.

Unperturbed, Anla and the skier looked bright-eyed at the long lines of breakers, curving gently along the shallow crescent of the beach, erupting in high, slow-falling spasms on the rocks of the promontory. The skier turned to Anla, ignoring Theri, obviously finding the silent woman in the cape the better bet—better looking, too, no doubt.

"They're breaking well today," he announced.

"Yes."

"They always do that with a southerly blowing, gives them a nice slow break."

"Don't you ever fall through?"

"Zee-gee. Cods, I've had some zee-gees all right. Field dephased once."

"Take in any water?"

"For a few seconds. Trouble is, I can't swim. Bloody near drowned."

"It sounds awfully dangerous."

"Yeah, well there's risks involved, of course. That's part of the fun really. Not that I'd deliberately do anything stupid, mind you, not with the rest of bloody eternity ahead of me, but I reckon if a thing's worth doing you've gotta be prepared to take a bit of a gamble. Know what I mean?"

"What about jaws?"

"Ah well, you see them cruising about occasionally, but they never touch you if you're in a field. Must reckon you're one of them."

"Are you?"

"Eh?"

"A jaw?"

The skier looked nonplussed for an interval, and gazed out to sea. At length his neck stiffened and he laughed meaningfully.

"Might have a bit of it in me."

Theri, having taken as much as she could stand, unrolled from her cocoon, turned off her library and walked slowly down the beach in search of Kael and Ben.

The men stood on an exposed rock shelf, their feet washed by the odd wave larger than the rest. Theri watched them bending over something in a pool, silhouetted against the ocean and the clouding sky.

She picked her way across the shelf; the rocks were spiky with crustaceans, the hollows flat and slippery with olive-green seaweed. Torpid, the thick tubular trunks awaited the incoming tide to swirl them alive again. The raped remains of bivalves clung in clusters, their inhabitants taken years ago by ecological competitors.

Ben and Kael were examining a small native polyp trapped in a pool. Ben was explaining the niceties of sea-food preparation:

"And then you peel off the tough outer skin and marinate it for two days in white grape wine and lemon juice, something citric anyway."

Theri considered the little animal; its tentacles were coiled loosely over each other, the three unblinking eyes in its bulbous head steadily regarding the aliens. "We're going to be hard pressed to eat that thing."

"Its amino acids are compatible."

"I realize that."

"The colonizing Million did, and they had no wine."

"They also ate jaws, if they weren't eaten first."

The little nest in the dunes was deserted, a lonely dump of filaments and still-bulging foils. Ben shrugged, unconcerned: "She must have gone for a walk in the other direction."

Theri made no mention of the oaf but started to help Kael unpack the prepared food modules. She twisted the tags, setting off the rapid chemical catalysis which had the vegetables steaming by the time Kael ripped the foils open. Ben gathered firewood: scraggy roots of dead scrub and driftwood.

"Can you see Anla yet?"

Theri rose, licking her fingers, and examined the empty curve of the beach, the desolate jumble of dunes. Coming over the scalp of a long, bald dune, Anla and the cretin appeared.

A confusion of mutinous velvet in the lee of her body, Anla's cloak clung skin-tight to windward. Her hair floated, a black flag above black sails. The laminar loon plodded beside her, a fish out of water.

Chariots almighty, Theri thought, aghast, she hasn't been having it off with that dimwit already! She can't have, it's too cold anyway. Hope the men scare him off.

Anla caught sight of Theri and raised an arm in comradely salute. She started down the slope of the dune with her doggie. Theri slid down to the smoky fire Ben was building.

"Anla's coming. She seems to have struck up a friendship with the skier."

Kael, guilelessly: "That's good, maybe he'll lend us his rig."

Ben said nothing.

Anla and the body-skier arrived. Theri looked at the man's feet sticking scowl-like out of the slick legs of his heat-suit. Several toes were missing. Munched by jaws, with any luck, or had he carelessly left them at home?

"Hello, this is Liff. This is Ben, my pair-bond, Kael and Theri."

Kael clasped hands, offering the skier a buzz, inviting him to eat, starting a conversation about wave mechanics. Theri sat on the sand and regarded them both with scornful ire. She detected a note of triumph in the confident argot of the skier.

If he hasn't scored with Anla already, she told herself, he bloody thinks he's going to. Christ in Britain, why does Kael have to chat up the sod? Why does Anla have to contract some sordid little affair with him? Why doesn't bloody Ben tell him to piss off? Sick, that's what they are, bloody sick. They're just scared. Kael's scared of making enemies, of unpleasantness, of admitting that sometimes people just hate each other on sight.

And Ben, bloody Ben's scared of being seen to compete for Anla, even though he knows he could only win. Too bloody proud to be seen to fight for his spouse. And Anla's just playing games for the sheer stupid fun of it. To prove to herself she has the power no one else doubts for a minute.

Why are my friends such bloody fuckwits?

§

The responsibility for discord resting lightly on her becaped shoulders, Anla gazed after Theri's dwindling figure; gone off in some childish huff because of Liffbabes here. We must all give our undivided attention to our own kind twenty-four hours a day apparently.

And Kael, over there, repressing his jealousy under a load of old bonhomie. He can't even pilot a commuting skite without total cybernet control, what's all this bullshit about sports models? Silly bugger, I'd trade fifty skiers for him any day.

As for you, my dearly beloved husband, it's about time you realized that this long suffering retreat into the black hole of your self-sufficiency will get you nowhere.

§

Ben poked the fire's smoldering ashes with a stick and told himself that he had been through it all so many times before. "I've been through it all so many times before," he muttered inaudibly.

He looked at himself from a distance. Here we have Ben who has known only Anla who has known so many. He ceased his mumbling and silently observed the usurping prickbearer who favored a certain rare class of wave, endorsed and actively pursued the individual acquisition of exchange-value, and would shortly be trading in his sportskite on a faster one. That exhausted Liff as a topic.

A sad dilemma, Ben thought. For he understood well enough

the fascination Anla must feel for the differing contours of the athlete's muscles.

Had not he himself, half awake on so many mornings riding the public rapid transit, eyed off the bare, stockinged or hinted legs of unknown women, trim thighs, under the most favorable conditions, disappearing only at the last moment into the shadow of their skirts? And chatted in a meaningless haze of lust at parties? Randy in the bug laboratory? Known the need to know the bodies of the myriad females who crossed and recrossed the daily circle of his sight? Here is Ben the unsure— but, he asked himself, unsure of what?

Not his "style" or his potency or his capacity. Indeed Anla has said he's very good at it, and she is not without the yardstick of comparison.

Nor does he dread the loss of face at having his advances rejected; he could hardly be rejected by those who plainly propositioned him, which had happened often enough. Ben decided, as often before, to screw the next available wom(an)(en).

I wish the fucking pest would just *piss off.* He rose without a word to wander about the beach.

§

Theri, her feet leaving minimal impression on the sand, wondered what would have happened had Catsize been present. Some stunt to goad Ben or Kael into action? Or an intervention on his own behalf? Outings sans Catsize usually seemed to go off at half-cock.

The four of them had "found" Catsize one evening not long after the marriage.

In the center of a recently-sprinkled common, the Revived Christer Commandos stood bearing witness to the new scientifically established date for their god's return. The prima facie issue was whether the millennium began on 1 Jan 4000 or the same day of 4001; a subsidiary question concerned the symmetry which supported 4004 as the specified date.

The troops were a semi-circle of blue and gold spangled with the gleam of silver harps. A massive bellied man stood ready to thump a drum that protruded from his waist like a tumor of heroic proportions. On a floater in the center of the arc their green-faced leader was beseeching the crowd in conclusion:

"...and if there are any of you here who wish to repent your sins, do not hesitate to kneel down and offer up your souls to Christ Jesus as many billions have done before this benighted era. Salvation in the bosom of Christ the Charioteer...."

The four of them joined the incredulous crowd around the band, bringing attendance up to two dozen, if you counted the buzzed-out pair of drunks swaying in hallucination. No likely converts here, unless one of the drunks was the type that saw God in his stone. Ben peered into the gaping mouth of a trombone clutched by a buxom commando lass with jaunty tendrils. In her free hand she held a library.

"...and now we shall sing hymn number two hundred and ten, Angels of grace Thy Chariots fly. Those of you who wish to join in, do not hesitate to do so."

The band addressed their instruments and punched their score codes, ready to blast and strum and tinkle forth. From the front of the crowd a petulant voice enquired: "Hey, Commander, how can we join in the songs if we don't know the words, eh?"

The leader turned to face the crowd, looking down from his floater at the petitioner. Catsize gazed up earnestly: "How can we praise the Lord our God if we haven't the words of the songs, Commander?"

"I take your point. I shall read you a couple of verses aloud— better still, maybe you'd like to read them out so everyone can hear."

The commander stepped from his floater and borrowed the library held by the buxom lass. He handed it to Catsize, who cleared his throat and prepared to speak, suddenly had a better thought and climbed onto the Christer's floater. Catsize began to read, earnestly, devoutly, slowly getting caught up by the spirit of the thing:

"O hear us when we cry to Thee for those in peril on the sea and on the land too, friends, as the tectonic plates creak on the foundations of the deep, and for those in the air like the fowl of the field and the hounds of the Baskervilles and all things bright and beautiful are called unto the Lord thy manufacturer for ever and ever or whichever comes earlier, yea verily. For lo and behold I say unto you, did he who made the lamb make thee? Answer me that if you can, you sinners and blasphemers, you godless, whoremongering scoundrels, for verily, verily, comrades and friends, I am the way and the light and don't you bloody forget it. For the time has come for a terrible fire to be on the land and visions come to me of the arsehole of the universe farting forth a mighty thunder. For Moses begat Jacob who begat Sodom who begat Tomorra and all creeping things, and let you who are without stones come forth and be multiplied. And if there's any of you here with sin in your hearts and minds, well, you just kneel down on the common like the man told you to, pronto quicksmart if I was you, there isn't much time left, you dunderheads."

During this diatribe the band stared in a mixture of shock and anger at the arrogator on the floater. The commander essayed a number of ineffectual exhortations of the that-will-do-you've-had-your-say-now type. Now he placed a restraining grip on Catsize's arm.

"Look you here, Generalissimo, you just unhand me, zinger, for verily I am a truth sayer come out of Andromeda, man, to clear away the light and broadcast the memes of wisdom in the hearts of all humankind, and woe betide any who cast me out of their temples. And let it not be said that the holy rolling shock troops stood in the way of the redemption of their fellow man, cobber. For look you here, there's a right band of fornicators and idlers that needs the word like a desert needs phosphate. For the rich man builded his house upon the eye of the needle that it might walk forty days upon the water...."

Under this onslaught, delivered at a steadily rising rate of words/min, the commando stood back. Catsize swung to face the crowd. The spirit of repentence was upon him:

"Now then, you lot, bend the knee, you rabble. On your knees you balling, blasphemous, uncharitable tax-gatherers and publicans groaning to God from Bolte. For the Lord will send lightnings and Egyptian ruth-resistant tumors before the night's out if there's no unstiffening of necks here, comrades. For the Lord thy God is an envious old bugger, visiting the sins of the living zingers on the bones of their forefathers, though since it's a Y-carried retribution the foremothers will generally be spared. You lot repent and look smart about it—"

By this time the burly drummer had unshouldered his instrument and was in consultation with the chief. They advanced as a thundercloud upon the prating little man. Just before they could lay hands on him, however, first Ben and then Kael fell to his knees on the common. Catsize pointed an accusing finger at the penitents:

"Yeah, that's right, you sinners, you just get down there and open up your hearts to de Man. Coz der ain't no way but de narrow way dat leads to glory, frens. All dem ot'er paths dey just lead up dat ole garden path fulla dem ole debbel weeds and thistles right to dem fary pits. Hallelujah! Holy Moley, king a de Empire, sold his wife for a gimbled gyre. For Thine is the Empire, the way, and the—"

Kael and Ben raised their faces to Catsize the redeemer, salvation shining in their eyes. Commander and drummer, taken aback by the precipitate conversions, finally closed on Catsize, hefted him bodily into the air and carried him out of the semicircle, to the cheers of the crowd. Catsize all the while continued to preach:

"...the transportation of the hosts, for on the third day he is risen, and the blood of the lamb streams in the infirmary like the gentle rain which droppeth not, neither doth it spin."

His words cut off the instant his feet touched the ground, a deactivated robot. He brushed the hair out of his eyes, handed the library back to the commando woman and waved a depreciative hand at Ben and Kael.

"Well, I've bagged a brace for you. I've seen better in my time but you'll have to make do."

Catsize disappeared. Kael and Ben stood up, rubbed at the grassy stains on their knees, and rejoined Anla and Theri. Slowly, still laughing in contagious gusts, they made their way across the common, turning by common consent into the first pub they came to.

"Have you no shame?" The prophet stared in outraged surprise. "Offering yourselves to God one minute and slinking into a common buzz house the next!"

Kael fought his way to the bar while the others, grinning with delight, sat down with the preacher, introducing themselves. Catsize had just come down from the tropics; he had been sleeping in his skite and was in need of somewhere to stay. He spent that night on the Griffiths' sofa. In the morning he started to clean out the ancient laundry, offering liberal use of his skite in lieu of rent.

§

Theri sat on a log thrown up by some particularly high tide. The wood was rough and coarse-grained, bleached almost white by the action of sun and salt.

It really was incredible that so many planets throughout the universe were so perfectly adapted to human life. You couldn't account for it on statistical grounds; there were just too many divergent ways for stellar and planetary evolution to jump. These worlds had been planted, as the Aorist Closures had been planted.

Not built, but directed with consummate skill and care in the direction that would suit Homo sapiens sapiens when his own home was wheezing under the strain. Ergo, the intervention of deity?

There seemed to be some outrageous theory doing the rounds at the moment that the Charioteers were humans from the deep future, supernally puissant, reaching back to the universal dawn with tachyon instruments akin to those that drove the Teleports, forging the foundations of their own history. Crazy stuff. But better than that vile Christer rubbish.

She ran her hand over the log's solid, abrasive surface. Thinking about Catsize had dissolved her anger; she felt detached from her friends, fatalistic about the outcome of their mutual relations.

She sought to divine the future for Anla and Ben, for Kael and herself, but no prediction came to her. Pity memetic biosis can't forecast individual lives. She shivered. No, no, no; that stochastic limitation was their only margin of freedom.

If anyone knew the future it would be Catsize, attune to intuitive rather than mathematical networks. She resolved vaguely to ask him sometime.

A kilometer away, Ben was walking slowly towards her. Theri looked at the sea and listened to the boom and roar of the surf. She would be glad of Ben's company, she realized, by the time he reached her, happy to talk to him if he were in the mood for talk, content to walk in silence if he were not.

She thought again of Catsize. He had been with Ben and Anla ever since that night. Sometimes he was employed, running freelance projections on his library, piloting a freighter, driving cleaning equipment at night. She was sure he could be wealthy if he felt like it. Sometimes he had short poems taken by Databank, and occasionally someone consulted them and he was paid his royalty. Usually he was on the dole.

Once he had disappeared and returned a few months later, brown and affluent. He had taken them all out to dinner, bought a handsome stash of premier intoxicants and some expensive clothes, "loaned" impoverished friends exchange-credit, paid for somebody's gene-job, and seemed pleasantly surprised to find himself broke within a month.

He appeared to do most of the cooking in the Griffith establishment. Certainly he was a better chef than Anla, whose culinary highpoint had been William Wool, and Ben—for all his theories about marinated polyped—would be hard pressed to sear an egg. He was a sort of human enzyme, a catalyst.

Catsize had helped found an inferential theatre troupe and eventually Ben had become a member, on a sporadic basis.

As Kael had pointed out, it was during his feuds with Anla that Ben took to acting, working it all out on the boards. Kael also maintained that Catsize had saved Ben and Anla's relationship. Maybe, Theri thought; a strange and strained salvation.

§

In the dunes, Kael, Anla and the body-skier continued to sit around the dead ashes of the fire.

Little was said. Anla had withdrawn into herself, finding no need at the moment for either of her companions; their times would come. Kael addressed the odd word to the skier, but seemed more interested in the maze-running abilities of a beetle for whom he had constructed, between his outstretched legs, a labyrinth in the sand.

The oaf, a man of few words and fewer interests, was nevertheless not one to relish reflective silences. Sensing no further point in hanging around, he spoke the formula of a hearty goodbye, glanced with a display of optic nudges at Anla, and made his way over the sand to the faulty Skyhog. A waterproof pocket of his heat-suit contained his library, in which, doubtless, were stored the ones and zeroes of Anla's code.

Moments later the Hog's modified drive sounded faintly above the noise of the waves and was gone.

Kael placed his forefinger a centimeter in front of the beetle, drew one decisive route to freedom through the imprisoning walls, and stood up.

Anla accepted his proffered hand. Together, they went in search of Theri and Ben.

PART SIX

1.

Two sub-graduates approached post-luncheon Kael from the far end of the corridor, the girl proctor and one of the lesser lights in the hierarchy, a boy from a well-placed bureaucratic Clan, their garments neat and wrinkle-free, their hair the hue prescribed by their genes, insignia of probity gleaming on the well-upholstered breast, the manly chest.

Ah, so, love in the corridors while the underlings cavort in the healthy urban air? Yearning glances in the uncommon stillness of the deserted labs?

Kael watched the highly glossed shoes walking in step towards him, while his own frontiersman's boots squeaked gently on the plast parquetry.

Alas, no. The girl proctor looked at Kael, seeking audience. He stopped. Young educer conferring wisely with senior pupils.

"Sensei, it's Con Ephores and his friends."

"What about them?"

"They won't go out, sensei."

"Well, they probably don't want to go out."

"But they're not supposed to be inside during luncheon."

"But *you're* inside during luncheon."

"But we are the proctors on duty."

"And it's your job to throw people like Con out?"

"Well, yes, sensei. They can only stay in if they have an educer's permission."

"Maybe they have."

"They can't have, they're in the holographic lab, writing visuals on the computer."

"Well, that's doing something isn't it? They're not breaking the place up, are they?"

"Sensei, they won't say what they're programming."

Kael tried not to laugh. "Look, if anyone objects, Con and his friends have my express permission to use the down-time facilities during luncheon. It's probably the only chance they get. They obviously have authorization for the running time or they wouldn't have been able to log in."

"If you say so, sensei."

Kael walked on down the corridor, past the den of iniquity. Con sat on a programmer's stool like a holly producer, leaning forward, expounded to Alexi. Two other boys Kael did not recognize, and the tubby little red-haired girl he'd seen at the Alliance, were bent over control panels.

A small monitor cube swirled with color, and a stiff cartoon figure solidified briefly. Kael thought he recognized the jerking manikin, and stifled a guffaw.

He waved as he passed; Con waved back and went on with his directing.

Kael entered the Sciences Staff room, an altogether more palatial establishment than the soft folks' room downstairs, bright, airy and smelling faintly of reagents. Two physicists were playing starwar on a console lanned to the same computer from which Con et al were stealing cycles. Neither was the man Kael wanted. They beckoned him over, and he drew up a stool.

He had all his battlecraft volatilized without scoring a point.

§

Kael retraced his steps, glanced again inside the media room. He paused at the door, watching in silence. Bathed in laser light, Anla stood flanked by the sub-graduate politburo. With firm professional authority she was saying, "If you haven't got permission, Con, I'm afraid you will have to go outside."

Con rested on his elbows, a man totally relaxed and at home in his world, despite the spartan comforts of his programmer's stool. The other three boys sat upright and uncomfortable, looking to their spokesman. The girl was running their work into a crystal; she'd turned the monitor cube off.

Con answered in his own time. "Madam Griffith, nobody else wishes to use the holo-system right now. It is fascists who prevent people from creating art. I thought you were meant to be a libertarian."

Anla over-reacted. "I couldn't care less about your tinkering. You can hire time on your home libraries whenever you like. Now go outside."

"On Kurd they burn people who seek access to the media of public expression. On Kurd, who will commune freely with a networked library when a secret policeman echelons each one?" Con gestured contemptuously at the proctors.

Anla spoke with a hard note of anger: "Con, will you and your friends go out now? It's a rule that you can't be inside the building at luncheon, and that's got nothing to do with what goes on in Kurd. Anyway, I'm very concerned about Kurd, I was almost arrested for petitioning last year," she ended rather lamely, "but that's got nothing to do with you lot being in here now."

Con slumped even further over the console, resting chin in cupped hand.

"Madam Griffith, you have all the political consciousness of a spayed grundle."

Anla took two quick steps into the room and glared down on Con, who assumed the demeanor of a man basking under a pleasant G-zero sun.

"Get out. Get out now!"

The rest of the group blinked in confusion; the girl, holding her programmed crystal protectively, glanced nervously at the proctors, who stared in righteous outrage at Con, who languidly raised an arm in salute to Kael.

Anla turned suddenly. Relief showed on her flushed face, replaced quickly for the benefit of the proctors by a look of competence and justified anger. The girl proctor's face revealed nervous embarrassment.

"Mr. Ponchard, will you tell Con and his friends to leave the building immediately."

Kael admired the rise and fall of Anla's breasts under her red knitted dress. Anla crossed is Anla sexy. He spoke with an exaggerated softness: "By no means, Anla, I can't see any good reason why they shouldn't be here, and neither can you."

The two proctors started visibly at this unprecedented breakdown of collective responsibility, at the taboo intimacy. Con's band relaxed a little. Anla looked steadily at Kael for a few seconds, her eyes bright and hard. When she spoke it was slowly, distinctly, every word given its precise dramatic emphasis:

"They haven't got permission to be here, Sensei Ponchard."

"On the contrary, they have my permission. Besides, I don't think the rule that forces them to go outside is very sensible, do you?"

Anla disregarded the question. "But they have told me themselves they haven't got permission."

"Quite so, they don't know about it; I only told these two, since they seemed so worried."

Anla stared at the two proctors. The girl blushed and looked at her immaculately shod feet, the boy maintained the blank idiot gaze he had worn from the start. "Why didn't you tell me this?"

"We didn't think it was proper permission. They should have asked before they stayed inside." She spoke to the floor.

Anla flashed Kael a look of pure hate and backed down as gracefully as the situation allowed.

"There seems to have been some misunderstanding, but in future, Con, you will have to get permission *before* you stay inside."

Con gave a single, enigmatic shrug. Anla turned quickly and marched out of the facility with the proctors close on her heels.

Kael watched the three representatives of law and order vanish down the corridor, then turned to Con.

"I won't ask what you've been up to, though I imagine I'll find out soon enough." He looked steadily at the youth. "Don't spread this story all over the place, will you, mate?"

"No worries."

§

Anla sat at the console of Catsize's skite, hyper-cool now, efficiently taking Kael and herself through the afternoon traffic. Kael lay well back in the passenger web, his feet up.

He looked down through the safety field at the arrays of flashy baubles: an estate of new cottages. All very neat. Designs chosen by the tenants.

Charioteers, the first colonists showed a bit more taste. Simplicity constrained by raw materials. Are they living in bliss today in these new horrors, glad, two and a half centuries later, to be out of the original whitewashed stone walls, mellow thatched roofs, twisting cobbled streets?

The uses of freedom. If the political consciousness of this community is on a par with its aesthetics we're all stuffed.

The silence in the skite's cabin was becoming oppressive.

When Anla spoke it was coolly, with no hint of aggression.

"It's very easy to do that sort of thing, Kael."

"What sort of thing exactly is that, Anla?"

"Feed your own image of yourself at the expense of the other staff."

"You think I sided with Con only for the benefit of my own ego?"

Anla didn't answer; she went to manual briefly, her option homeostatting into the cybernet, and slid deftly up into the highest corridor.

"Listen Kael, leaving the stolen computer time to one side, I don't give a fuck whether Con and his friends break that stupid rule or not. If I can turn a blind eye to it I will, and so will a lot of other educers around the place. But if it comes to a direct question, as it did when those bloody proctors asked me to enforce the rule, I have no choice."

Kael sat up in his web and shrugged, seeing the line Anla's argument must necessarily take. He looked down at the muddy river flowing sluggishly under the equally sluggish line of skites. A gray sky, more rain coming. The next question, and its answer, were inevitable; he was constrained to ask it:

"Why did you have no choice?"

Anla chose her words with care.

"Because educers have to function as a group, as a team, if you don't mind the word. You have to live with your fellows, you depend on them for all kinds of support. You have to be able to trust them and they have to be able to trust you."

"Bullshit!"

"Don't be so bloody petulant, Kael, you know what I'm saying is true."

"Don't you really mean that you were scared of what Con was programming on that holo?"

"Of course I'm worried, Kael. Con's a smart kid, and I know he's only five or six years younger than us but for all that he's just a child. He's impatient, he'll destroy himself if someone doesn't slow him down for a few years—"

"Yet you didn't confiscate their crystal."

"Don't be offensive, you can see the difference as well as I can. Besides, they'd just go ahead with their little scheme some other way. On the other hand, now the proctors know they're up to something they'll put it aside if they have any sense at all. But that's not the point. I repeat: if we educers start embarrassing and contradicting each other in front of the kids, we fuck up any chance of mutual support, and the whole job becomes impossible."

The flow had speeded up. Kael turned his attention to the dwellings again; they were deep in the airspace of the established bureaucracy.

How the nimby swine had shrieked when the press of traffic

had forced the opening of this corridor. Tall trees edged the bland translucence of privacy fields. What mad, illicit scenes raged beneath their cover?

Kael wondered who would get thrown out first, he or Con, and found the form fairly equal.

Of course Anla is right, he told himself, depressed. The job would very soon become impossible. Maybe for me it already has.

§

Theri sat on Catsize's bed, listening to the thornglee outside flailing around in an orgy of mutual mutilation. Rain droned across the roof of the laundry. The poet threw a few lumps of compressed tea into the urn and activated it. Theri pulled a filament over her knees.

"Catsize, do you have any kids?"

"Half the universe has been sired by my mighty pizzle, child."

Catsize swore by natural combustion; he selected a few fragments of driftwood Ben had fetched back from the ocean, and sprinkled a chemical catalyst over them. The wood caught with a rush of flame, filling the room with a sudden marigold light. Theri watched the flames shattering in the rain-streaked windows of the Cathouse. Outside, the gray afternoon had almost turned to night. A sunlight went on in the main dwelling; Anla or Ben must be home.

"What do you think will happen to them?"

Catsize warmed his hands over his primitive fire and looked at Theri.

"It will depend what happens when Ben finally starts to screw around like Anla. I think when it comes down to it our Ben is a one-woman-at-a-time man. Reacting against his upbringing. He'll probably start to have it off with some wench to teach Anla a lesson and then find he's up to his ears in love with her and want to leave Anla."

"What will Anla do?"

"Go berserk, I should imagine; she really needs Ben. She loves him, too."

"Do you think they'll break up?"

"No. At least not for long, Anla's far too strong to just let Ben go wandering off with some other woman—she'd get him back after a month or two."

"When do you think it'll happen?"

"Fairly soon, probably. With any luck it should bring them both to their senses."

"Is she screwing that body-skier?"

"She was for a week, then he disappeared, she must have pissed him off. About bloody time too, what a pest.... Funny thing about Anla is that she sometimes tries to get Ben off with some nice little dolly or other. Of course, she never picks anyone who could possibly be a long-term rival. I wouldn't mind betting that's what keeps Ben so embarrassingly faithful to her; he's hardly going to race off some lusty as an act of defiance if Anla's actively encouraging him from the sidelines. She's perceptive, in an intuitive sort of way."

Theri unwrapped herself and poured the tea. Catsize was watching the fire spreading little petals of flame along a bent leg of driftwood; the planes of his face flickered. She handed him his potion.

"Catsize, why aren't you like this more often?"

"How do you mean?"

"Like you are now, not acting. Not performing."

"What makes you think I'm not acting now?"

"Because you've been talking seriously and making sense."

Theri retired to the bed and pulled the filament over her knees again. Catsize drank from his mug and placed it on the floor at his feet.

"Do you believe I can't act at being serious and sensible? Here I am, in front of my fire, watching the universe with ancient eyes that have seen it all before, telling the very truth to my faithful disciple. Tiresias and his charge—an excellent role for a wet night."

Theri laughed uncertainly, and then caught her breath. Catsize aged, his sight fading, hunched in his chair, holding his hands to the fire and slowly unbending the joints of his arthritic fingers, searching in vain for the lost warmth of youth. It was the mistaken horror of the ancient myths: immortality without rejuvenation. Fire light gave half his face a stolen, demonic life.

"Catsize, dear, have you foresuffered all?"

"A good part of it."

"How old are you?"

"Timeless, ageless."

"Catsize, do you know what is going to happen to me and Kael?"

"Of course."

"Tell me."

"It's best you don't know, my child."

2.

Rubbing at her temples, Anla wondered yet again why she had so much trouble sleeping. It was obviously psychogenic; cloned offspring were free of ontogenetic mishaps, the quality control systems saw to that, and Jard's chromosomes had been mapped for deleterious mutations as a matter of course.

Ben was still glooming around in the aftermath of that dumb fucking skier. He'd usually pulled himself together by this stage.

Her eyes skimmed the master console, watching how her kids scored on their "elicit-and-anchor" schedule. A striped pink bar moved up Streb's readout, indicating too much alpha in his EEG. Before the autonomics had a chance to hit critical and give him a boot in the tail, with loss of points recorded toward his semester total, Anla cut in her voice circuit.

"Wake up, Streb, it's no wonder you have a memory index like a sieve."

The kid jerked out of his daydream, blushing, and fixed his eyes on the mnemonic schematics twitching away in the holo field. She hoped the kid wasn't fantasizing about her.

A tone sounded; all the children dropped their eyes to the questions coming up on their libraries and stabbed away as best they could.

I wonder how Kael is hacking it, she thought, slugging with his class in that rotten little room they've stuck him in half a kilometer from everyone else. She remembered her own first year at Curringal, one of the untouchables at the bottom of the status ladder, given a room with defective heating, tramping twice as far as anyone else to get to her class.

She hadn't remained untouchable for long; silly old Vann'd had his hands on her within days. Special treats in the Senior Commissary, the move to a superior classroom closer to the comforts of civilization.

Duvid's readout blipped. That kid must have suet for brains; give him the entire peptide schema from Victoria's leading geographer and he'd still get lost crossing the common. Anla cut him out of the programmed interrogation and asked him gently what he'd forgotten.

His miserable face stared up at her, lower lip thrust out and eyes brimming.

"Never mind, dear, we'll have it sorted out in a moment, won't we? Now where—"

"Attention, class!"

Anla was washed by abrupt, scalding rage. Shit! As if this job wasn't delicate enough, without some cretinous busybody disrupting the kids' concentration.

"The Co-ordinator of Curringal Basic Inlay will now speak to you on a matter of the gravest importance."

Jonga Hewson, bloody old Grey's simpering right hand, vanished from the holo field. The embodiment of sagacity took her place, seated behind his massive console.

Anla turned away, her jaw locked, and began putting the readouts on temporary stand down. Blocking her own attention, she only vaguely heard the voice saying with gray anger: "It has come to my notice as head of this establishment it has come to my it has come to my notice that an organized group of come to my notice that—"

The voice broke off, and Anla looked up with some surprise. What was the old fool on about? He was glaring at the class of small children. "In this institution, all political organizations are banned. It has come to my notice that an underground, covert group of troublemakers is at work in Curringal, and I will not tolerate it. Although we do not know the names of those involved, it is said that pupils can easily contact them simply by asking around."

That's funny, Anla thought. There's something weird about— And then she realized who Grey was talking about. Those bloody snotty-nosed little proctors must have taken Con's infractions to the top.

"Let me make this perfectly clear," the gray man was saying with rising wrath. "There is a Departmental ruling which clearly forbids the discussion of all controversial issues in class. Your educers are forbidden to discuss Imperial guerrilla wars even if they want to. This underground group, which claims to be upholding the banner of freedom against what it calls the foul abuses of bureaucratic power, is carrying on in direct defiance of the Defense Forces Protection Act."

Chariots on ice, he's flipped his lid! Grey's bilious voice was verging on hysteria. Anla glanced at her charges; they were staring with wide eyes. Most of this was going over their heads, but they recognized the authentic tone of maddened fury. The bastard, he'll have them in tears in a moment.

"I have just one final thing to say. Next week the Imperial Legation will be arriving on Victoria from Earth, and people will make their traditional representations. I know for a fact— for a fact! that this rabble of secret conspirators plans to turn that public gathering into a riot. Such a riot can only succeed if everyone who agrees with their criticism joins them outside the Teleport in Bolte on that day. And I forbid it! I forbid it!"

Anla stared at the three-dimensional, frothing image with total incredulity. Breathing hoarsely, Grey's projection looked out on them with crazy eyes. In the silence, someone at the back of the room blew a loud raspberry.

Anla lurched forward on her console and gazed numbly at her petrified group. There wasn't one of them who would have made that sound. Charioteers, they were only ten years old! A strangled scream came up from the holo field.

"Stand up the child who did that! Stand up I say!"

"I didn't," an infant wailed, bursting into tears; her protestation was drowned by a chorus of cries. "Ooooh! Madam, look!"

Spinning back, Anla saw that the livid co-ordinator had spasmed to his feet. His face had turned, literally, green. He wore no trousers.

Anla uttered one appalled shriek of laughter. She toggled the projector *off*; it remained on. Over-ridden. Oh Con, you fucking lunatic! She strode briskly to the door and threw it open.

"All right, children, into the corridor. Come on now, one two three. That's right, Streb, out you go. Now I want you all to march down to the playroom like good little children and wait for me there. Pronto!" She clapped her hands. Did they have a lanned holo-projector in the playroom? Well, once they were down there someone else could take charge. She waited until they had straggled off, then ducked back into the class room.

Grey had shrunk to half-size, and he was wearing the full regalia of an Imperial Commando general, without the trousers. A shocking detail struck her: between his legs the flesh was smooth. Co-ordinator Grey was, as she'd always claimed, completely dickless.

Anla blinked, amazed, at the brilliant double-bind the image represented. At least they wouldn't be able to prosecute the kids for lewdness and obscenity.

An idealized boy pupil entered the frame, all sinew and revolutionary fervor but polite with it, did a double-take and ventured toward the jerking, babbling manikin with the clear intention of announcing that the emperor wore no clothes. The diminutive tyrant seized up an explosive grenade and blasted the boy to bloody rags.

Chariots, Con, you're over-doing it a bit.

Now the background was Kurd, reconstructed from the eidetic schema of official news observers. Smoking ruins, rotting flesh: the victims of para-viruses.

Grey swelled to a bloated toad. "It has come to my notice," he screamed in a high-pitched voice, "that some pupils at Curringal Basic Inlay are changing the color of their hair. This will not be tolerated! I am the co-ordinator of this establishment."

Amid a series of disgusting farts, billowing clouds of horrid cartoon vapor swirled about the gargoyle. Grey blanched and ran about foolishly trying to seize them and stuff them back whence they had come.

Come off it, Con, Anla thought, discomfited. Surely we can expect a touch of taste and discretion even in propaganda. But through the walls, she could hear gales of laughter, yells, stamping feet.

How the hell had this pirate splice been allowed to go on for so long? They must have jammed the deactivation circuits in the entire lan.

She took up her library and punched Kael's code. Inactive. She tried two others. Both dead. Chariots, they've been thorough. And what has bloody Kael done? He's probably got his class taking notes on it.

The holo fizzed out. Someone had cut central power.

§

When order was restored Kael sat for a moment, getting his own reactions under control.

Press on with the scheduled subject matter, pretend nothing had happened? Absurd. Worse, it'd be passing up a rare chance to lead them into an exploration of something real, something relevant to their own experience.

The mood of the class suffered a phase change as he sat there; the psychic temperature dropped suddenly, their manic hilarity jerking downward into frightened, quiet expectancy.

"Well," Kael said, regarding them as calmly as he could, "what did you all think of that?"

Dead silence.

"Angelo?"

"The kids that done it will get expelled, won't they, sensei?"

"If they're caught. Do you think they ought to be expelled, Angelo?"

"Aw yeah!"

"Why, Angelo?"

"Well, they want to destroy Curringal, don't they, sensei?"

"Who else thinks that the people who programmed the holly want to destroy Curringal?"

A confused general babble, and some revived tittering. "It didn't show respect, did it, sensei?"

"No, Helee, whatever else it did, it didn't show respect."

"Well, they should of, even if they don't agree with Mr. Grey and that."

"Do you think they'll get caught, sensei?"

The whole class started to talk at once. Their confused fright was turning back into animation. Noise level rose sharply; Kael tried for some semblance of order.

"Look, do you think we ought to have a class debate about this?"

A couple of dozen voices: "Yes."

"No." Janelle in the front row.

"Don't you think it was important, Janelle?"

"This is meant to be a history search, sensei."

"Don't you think this has something to do with history?"

"There won't be a question on it in the exam, will there?"

"Oh dry up, you old bag. Don't listen to her, we want a debate."

"Sit down, Oni, Janelle has a right to her opinion and this *is* meant to be a search on galactic monetary development."

"Well, she can go and read her library if that's all she cares about."

"Don't get so excited, Oni. If most of you want a debate

there's no reason why those who don't can't go and work by themselves on a library. Who apart from Janelle doesn't want a debate?"

Silence.

Janelle grabbed up her library and made a rush for the door.

"She's just like that, sensei, a real goody-goody. All she thinks about is passing exams."

"All right, all right, you lot. It took Janelle more courage to be the odd-one-out than most of you've got." Kael listened with amazement to his own sententious phrase—the real educer's touch. "Right, now who's going to be chair?"

"You, sensei."

"No, one of you lot will have to be, I'm tired of doing all the work around here."

As Kael was about to vacate his place in favor of Jo, the appointed chair, the door opened and Janelle scuttled to him. "What is it, Janelle, do you want to come back to the debate?"

The girl mumbled something; she looked steadfastly at her feet and twisted her library. The class offered a number of derisive opinions. Kael ignored them, concentrating on Janelle. "What's the matter, dear?"

Again the child said something inaudible and continued to twist the machine in her red, sweaty fingers. Kael realized she was close to tears. Had the obscenity shaken her this badly? It might be better to cancel the debate.

He led her into the corridor and shut the door. Contemptuous comments penetrated to the echoing space stretching away to either side of them. "Now, what's the matter?"

"Need permission." The girl choked back a sob.

Hell, it'd be hopeless dragging her back in now, the others'd never settle down to a lesson, they'd take it out on her later. Kael pulled out his library and punched through authorization for the girl to use the big full access libraries at a time other than that specified by the time-table.

Janelle sniffled something that might have been, "Thanks," and hurried down the corridor. Could he have said anything to cheer her up? He returned to the class. Jo was sitting at Kael's station.

"Well, haven't you started yet?"

"We were waiting for you, sensei."

"What the hell for? You're chair, aren't you?"

Kael walked to the back of the class and eased himself behind Jo's console. She shouted for order. "Right, now I want someone to speak in favor of what we saw."

Silence, then whispering. Muttered entreaties filled the room. Kael wondered why the authorities hadn't appeared yet on the holo with a counterblast. Presumably Con and his mad friends had contrived to lay the system waste behind them.

"You speak."

"No, you."

"Tell Oni to."

All faces finally turned to Oni, child of a space-freighter crew; she rose to take her rightful place as rebel and general stirrer.

"Well, I think this is the best thing that's happened at Curringal since the time they tried to burn the commissary down."

"That was an accident, you dill."

"How would you know, you little twat?"

Jo banged Kael's master console. "Stick to the point, Oni."

"Well, I'm fed up with being told what to do all the time. Being told my hair isn't the right color by old Hewson. What does it matter to her what color my hair is? You never tell anybody off about their hair, do you, sensei? Well, what that program said is that people like Mr. Grey and Madam Hewson shouldn't be educers unless they can mind their own business. They won't let you leave the grounds at luncheon to buy eggs and chips, no, you've got to stay and go to the commissary where there's only a millionth of a centimeter of marg on the rolls—"

"What's that got to do with old Grey farting all the time?"

In the ensuing uproar, Jo struggled to get order. "Sit down, Oni, you've said enough to start off 'In Favor'. And you shut up,

Angelo, that was just a simulation, it wasn't real farting, I bet he never does. Order! Order! Tell 'em all to shut up, sensei."

Laughing, Kael said: "Quiet, the lot of you. If we're going to have a debate, you've got to listen to the speakers and do as the chair says. Okay, Jo."

"Right, now who's going to say something against the program. Helee?"

"Well, I think it's disgusting and I hope the kids who did it get arrested for treason."

"You would."

Jo waxed authoritative: "Shut up, Oni, you've had your go."

"What it showed Mr. Grey doing was real rude and he never would. Anyway he's co-ordinator, so he must be real good at his job, otherwise he'd just be an ordinary educer."

The class cringed in various degrees at this eulogy, but no one interrupted. Oni appeared now to be absorbed in study, a rare phenomenon. Helee rushed on: "And as for all that stuff about Kurd and everything, well, what's that got to do with getting your inlays? If the kids that did that don't even care if we get invaded one day, well, that's got nothing—"

"Please sensei, he's coming."

Imon squinted through a hole from his lookout post on the row of consoles next to the corridor.

"Who's coming, Imon?"

"Mr. Grey, sensei."

Strike me pink, a visitation in the flesh. Kael looked at his class; they were completely mute. Jo leapt to vacate the seat of power.

"I think we'd better have a proper program, sensei."

"Yes, sensei, Mr. Grey would be real mad. Like it said on the holly, you're not allowed to discuss controversial topics."

With a sigh, audible to all his tongue-tied pupils, Kael handed Jo's desk back and walked to the front of the room, taking his rightful place in the scheme of things. He looked at the class; the class looked at him.

"Well, while we're waiting let's talk about the fiscal exchange of eidetic data-blocks as a basis for—"

The gray man entered. The class got quickly to its feet. Kael rose very slowly to his. There were no salutations.

"Sit down, 3C, Mr. Ponchard. The public outrage of a few minutes ago calls for immediate action. I presume it was received on the class projector, and that you were unable to turn it off?" Kael nodded. Turn it off? Never occurred to me, mate, not in a million years. "I don't think any members of your class were directly concerned, it is doubtless the work of the overgrown louts and hussies in pre-graduate. I expect all of you unwittingly witnessed some of that vile performance. First, let me make perfectly clear that those responsible will be severely dealt with. I trust that none of you needs to be told that the entire exhibition was a vile concoction...."

Kael stood slightly behind the gray man and listened to the practised anger of a century or more, climbing to a parody of the parody.

Grey neck rose, faintly flushing, from gray ruff to the rigidly defined line of fake gray hair. Well, if the whole bloody incident has done nothing but prove the bugger a mammal rather than a mutated reptile something has been achieved.

Kael looked at his pupils: thirty-five stolid recipients of this authentic bit of emotion, seventy eyes fixed on the gray man but not, it would seem, on his face. If telekinesis was a fact they'd drill a hole through his sternum.

Kael suddenly felt the absurdity of the whole situation. Here I stand behind the back of this ranting lunatic, with a serious expression on my face, befitting the gravity of the matter in hand. The iron-gray General and his loyal aide-de-camp. Suppose I were to do a little soft-shoe, stand on my hands, thumb my nose at the back of old grayness, pull down my own pants, fart a couple of times?

An involuntary smile crossed Kael's face. He caught himself and repressed it.

What if I were to bond a notice saying "Do Not Feed The Reptile" to his back and send him off so labeled to wind up his voyage of retribution? Or a holo patch showing a foaming dog.

The desire to laugh got worse. He broke into a quick grin. He set the muscles of his face and stifled a giggle in his throat. He glanced at his charges but they were all looking at the gray man.

Suppose I were to tap him on the shoulder and inform him that I was making a citizen's arrest under the suppression of rabid dogs act?

Kael caught Oni's eye. She, too, was fighting an internal battle. A companion in this sort of fight is the last thing you want. He turned his back, abandoning Oni to her own struggle.

The gray words were building to a climax:

"...be certain of one thing, if there is a recurrence of this disgraceful incident the whole student body will suffer. So it is in your own interests that whoever is responsible is brought to light. Thank you, Mr. Ponchard, I regret the need to have interrupted your program like this."

Kael turned just in time to meet the gray man's eyes as he left the room. "Not at all, Mr. Grey."

The door shut.

From the back of the room Oni's giggle ran cleanly through the silence.

"That will do, Oni, just calm down and stop...."

Oni put her head on her console and howled. Someone said in a high squeaky voice, "With his pants down." Kael's minimal defenses collapsed. He abandoned himself. Out of control, he found himself roaring and weeping with laughter. His diaphragm hurt and his eyes were awash with tears. Beyond his own laughing came the gale and then the hurricane of the kids' mirth.

§

Catsize looked incredulously at Mr. Smeeth.

"But didn't you tell this Inspector-General chappie about my size? I'm too frail for manual work."

"He thinks you're qualified for an office library."

"An office! But I'm a poet. Poets die in offices. Ruth can't save them, they wilt, they wither, and then they die. Pitiful it is, pitiful. I've seen it often through the centuries."

"He also talked to Schafschank about you."

"The fiend!"

"Keep your voice down. The Medbank dumped its high core and they traced it to your file. It seems you've been suffering from diseases extinct for millennia."

"It's me age! A wreck of a man right from the word go, and I mean the day J. Peter White skidded through a cow turd into the first Aorist Closure. I've been eaten by cancers, tumors, ague, pox, fever—"

"All right, all right, keep your voice down."

"And they want to condemn me to die in some hell hole of invoices and dear person re yours of the thirty-first instant it has come to our computer's attention that notwithstanding your update sincerely yours department of sprocket tighteners. Have they no shame! no soul, no—"

Aghast, Smeeth implored the ruined poet. "Look, just do me a favor, will you? just go along to these people and give them a try, just so as I can have it on my records that you've had a go—"

"You don't understand. I'm at a very crucial point in my art, I'm preparing a poem to welcome the Imperial Legation. This might be my chance to obtain sponsorship from the Court."

"I didn't know that!" Smeeth was impressed. He activated Catsize's file readout and searched the bright lines. "But it says nothing here about an official parliamentary invitation to—"

"No, it's sort of a freelance thing, you know, the spirit of Victoria speaks up from the crowd of petitioners."

Smeeth pulled at his chin. "Look, there's no real problem, you won't have to start your duties for a couple of weeks, and they probably won't take you anyway, and even if they do there'll be plenty of time to write poetry between the tea breaks. If the Legates are impressed by your poem you'll be all right anyway, and if not—though I'm sure they will be—you can get yourself fired after a year or two and come back and see me."

"It is a far, far better thing that I do, than I have ever done."

"I've read that poem too."

"Don't kid yourself, Smeeth, you've only vid the cartoon."

§

Kael and Anla stepped from the staff slide into an afternoon ablaze with noon light. Kael squinted, shielding his eyes with his library.

Efficient youths in earpads strode the lava between Curringal's trizzy dodecahedrons. Laser mirrors scorched from the roofs of media skites, nodding on their swivels like rows of roosting Phoenix birds.

Anla turned her head aside as someone aimed a big pickup at them.

"Not a word, Kael," she muttered. "What are these bastards doing here anyway, they'll never get permission to 'cast a report on this."

A smooth-voiced, beautiful woman stood in front of them. "Hello, you're educers from Middle Inlay, aren't you? You have any comments on this morning's extraordinary events?"

Anla tightened her mouth and pushed past. Kael saw flustered Madam Hewson, corralled a few meters away, open hers and say, "It was disgusting and I hope those who were responsible are expelled and convicted." He looked back at the media.

"Sorry love, we're just cleaners, must rush now."

"But aren't you Sensei Kael Ponchard, a first-year novice educer?"

Kael stared at her. "How the hell do you know who I am? We've never met have we?"

"Isn't it true that you gave permission to the culprits to use the facilities here in programming their attack on the Co-ordinator?"

Flabbergasted, Kael said: "The culprits?"

"At this moment a group of sub-graduates led by Con

Ephores is being interrogated by the Co-ordinator and members of the planetary militia. Do you deny your implication in their actions?"

In the shadow of the gathering crowd of support techs, Kael suddenly made out the red face of the girl proctor. She looked away and scuttled off with her tugging friends. Anla stood beyond the ring of recording equipment; she jerked her head at him imperatively.

A dizzying sense of absolute freedom gusted through Kael's body; he was light-headed, yet totally aware of every texture touching his skin, of the cold wind, the shafts of perfect light. Before he could speak burly Olp Scrancher was at his side, gesturing angrily at the media.

"Get out of here, you're trespassing on Departmental territory. Go on, woman, move your equipment, on the double."

Kael found himself plucked into shadow. Scrancher told him: "Come and have a buzz, old son. It's been a hectic day for all of us." He looked sideways at Kael. "For a moment there I thought you were going to stick up publicly for those louts. They'll be sent down in disgrace, you know, they'll be doing manual work for the rest of eternity."

Intoxicated in the chilly breeze, Kael laughed. "That'll make little Helee Horkins in 3C happy."

"Kael, my friend." Scrancher stopped in front of his skite and regarded him sadly, "Kael, lad, you haven't been discussing this thing with the kids, have you?"

"Of course. We had a debate about it—"

"You mean they saw the entire production? You didn't send them out of the classroom?"

"Olp, if Con and his friends are going to be sent down they deserved an audience for their pains at least."

"I see. You watched it with the kids, and then you sat down with them and had a heart to heart discussion about whether Sam Grey is actually a psychotic power maniac." Olp shook his head in sorrowful disbelief.

"Well, we started to, the kids broke it off when they heard the old man doing his rounds."

"At least somebody's got some sense."

They climbed into the skite. Catsize's borrowed vehicle, Anla at the controls, had already gone.

"You may have knackered yourself, old son," Olp told him. The skite lifted. "Now what was all that crap about you 'being implicated'?"

§

The soap-opera came to what was presumably meant to be a cliff-hanging end for the night. Ben threw himself into a chair and hollered: "News coming up". Theri entered the Griffith living room with a tray of coffee mugs, handed them around and sat silently on the floor at Kael's feet, leaning her head against his knee. Catsize was out for the night, perhaps getting stoned off his skull. He'd left a note announcing Smeeth's apostasy and his own conversion to Entropic Shaitanism.

"And now the alarming story of Con Ephores, the Bolte child who was suspended from Basic Inlay late this afternoon along with five fellow sub-graduates. Ephores masterminded what authorities dub 'a seditious and obscene provocation, critical of education in particular and Imperial society in general'."

Ben looked at his wife. "I thought you said they wouldn't dare 'cast anything about this?"

"I was wrong wasn't I?" Anla put her mug down with a jolt, spilling coffee. "Shit, of course. It's the Legation. This is a sort of lesson in miniature. They must be more worried than we've hoped for."

"Shhh!"

A brief clip from the cartoon's most innocuous segment was cavorting through the holly field. It was cut smartly, and the corner of the living room took on the semblance of Curringal's mechfab grouprooms viewed at a distance. Kids rushed out of the doors, noticed the out-of-field media skites, pointed and stared.

The angle changed. Educers stepped out wearily, faces averted. Two of them were Kael and Anla. They walked into the field, Anla quickly muttering something inaudible. Madam Hewson appeared, doing her emotional number. The scene cut to the Coordinator's office. Grey sat behind his enormous console, stern and parched.

"We asked Co-ordinator Grey what steps would be taken to ensure—"

Kael felt the muscles of his shoulders relax. He tousled Theri's hair. "Well, they censored that bit. Must have decided it was slanderous."

The segment closed with a long shot of Con and his fellow conspirators being marched out of the grounds. It was impossible to make out their features. Not a word had been heard from them.

Kael closed his eyes. Grey would hardly let the matter rest there. "Let's find Catsize and get stoned," he said.

PART SEVEN

The spaghetti bar was almost deserted. Another table held half a dozen people wearing jaunty Imperial colors, also stoking up for the coming exercise in participatory democracy.

"What's going to happen, Kael?"

"Don't know. If they're worried enough they'll be bound to schedule a downpour to dampen enthusiasm. Bit rough on the loyalists though."

Theri tore at her roll. "This thing's only got a millionth of a centimeter of marg on it." They both laughed. She speared her spaghetti, twisting a little whirlpool in the tangled sea of veggie sauce and pasta, and watched Kael finish his lurid green lasagna. He seems happy and relaxed, she though, but then he always is in restaurants and autocafes and pubs. He ought really to live on one of the old worlds, where they go in for the civilized thing in a big way.

Kael ordered coffee and started doodling on his library.

"What's that?"

"Design for a house."

"Who for?"

"I don't know, just thought I'd design a house."

Theri watched Kael sketching in the walls and doors of his house, while the CAD program rectified the stresses and tensions and pointed out ergonomic defects. She wondered if he was hoping for a full scale downpour so that they could abandon the event and go visiting instead. But of course everyone else would be at the Teleport.

"What do you want to do?"

"Eh? Aren't we going to the assembly?"

"Yes, but what would you really like to do?"

"Go to bed with you and a stash of stone."

Theri smiled, gripping his knees with hers under the bench. Kael expunged his architecture and authorized the tab. He helped Theri into her fur jacket.

The sky lay across the urban buildings like a wet rag. Spruced up for the occasion, the grass of the common bounced under their feet. They walked in step up the hill towards the Gardens, arms locked around each other.

Theri glanced sideways at Kael. He was wearing a black oilskin over a dusty-red jumpsuit. A warning drizzle began. His hair slowly turned darker, starting to cling to the up-turned collar of the oilskin. She thought he looked like a frontier fisherman.

He ought to be wearing sea-boots, she thought. Those soft things of his will soak up the water like salt.

They crossed to the Gardens. Drizzly haloes circled the glo-panels and the trees reflected a wet green light.

§

The crowd was still in its formative stage, a scatter of groups: threes, tens, scores, serving as nuclear clusters for odd individuals or pairs to attach themselves to, or to wander off from, free electrons, to be reabsorbed into other groups. Only the covert cops stood around singly—inert atoms, incapable of the chemical bonding that was building the crowd up around them.

It would be depressing, Kael thought, to arrive alone in this crowd, knowing nobody, whatever the strength of one's sympathy with its numerous causes. Presumably even the militia must have their own network of comradeship, the shared cold-eyed cop glance.

Kael told himself that his perspective was getting slightly paranoid. Most of these people were sturdy loyalists, here as much for the spectacle and pageant as for the phatic expression of their sectional interests.

He and Theri walked between the clusters, exchanging salutations with citizens they'd never seen before and might never see again, agreeing that certainly somebody must have botched the weather and there'd be hell to pay. They resisted absorption until they sighted the Alliance.

The group stood under a dripping tree, shielded by a portable rain field. Anla was laughing at something with Mart. Theri greeted everyone warmly, engaging Dav in a playful bearhug. Dav lifted her clear of the grass, gave a final squeeze and dropped her to the ground. Theri passed easily into the group's compass.

Kael felt the pull, the blind chemical valence. Dav slipped him a sonic grenade. Bemused, he handled the thing for a moment, then nearly dropped it. It was not a toy. This thing could rupture ear-drums, and worse.

He caught Anla's eye; she was watching him quizzically.

"Ready for action, Kael?"

He handed the low-level weapon to her.

"You can have it, Anla, I'm off to find my friends the underdogs."

He left the Alliance, his accelerated pulse beginning to slow, and went in search of banished Con and the conspirators.

The crowd had started to congeal. It was getting harder to pass between the laughing groups, and the groups swelled. In the festive mood, the drizzle was discounted.

Was this, in turn, some ploy of the psychodynamicians, a soupcon of adversity to anchor memories of the Emperor's emissaries and a vital, wonderful evening? Do you know, Mavis, one of my group actually *spoke* to one of them, really, from Earth!

Well, not that exactly; if the Legates did turn up at Bolte on the 1-in-128 roulette spin of indeterminate targeting, Kael knew, they'd come out in an ambulance, with the tatters of their artificial cloned support organs hanging like soiled cloth from their bodies. They would hardly be in a fit state to talk to anyone, let alone grant their petitions. But the ceremonial circumstances would have done the job for them. Everyone loves a parade. Everyone loves a facade.

For a moment, Kael found himself wondering, with horror, what it would be like to teleport halfway across the universe in a single jump. Fifteen days of total sensory isolation, metabolism eating your own flesh, mind locked into metatime hallucination.

Not much fun, fellas. I guess you earn your keep at the Emperor's table.

Theri at his side, Kael found himself on the outside of the crowd. Under the thin soles of his damp shoes he felt the rough surface of a road, remnant of the great thoroughfare laid down by the first Million on Victoria. Across the road uniformed police were assembling: vans and riot wagons, just in case, and rough lines of blue-flickering personal rain shields.

Artificial light gleamed on the silver-encrusted transduction mask of an officer efficiently organizing his men and women on a subvocal command circuit. Kael doubted that there were more than a hundred of them, but then the balance of the troops were probably still dining and would be airlifted in.

He stood on the edge of the merry crowd and studied the cops.

The officer with the silver trim directed a thin line of militia onto the steps of an old government building that fronted the Gardens.

A contingent of augmented commandos arrived; each had a synaptic goose hanging at his belt.

More petitioners were arriving in steady streams from various quarters. All were on foot; private skites were banned for the night.

Kael caught sight of Con, the red-haired girl and a dozen other kids passing behind the main body of police. They skirted a gliding van and crossed the road in a straggling file, holding up the free passage of another van for at least ten seconds. One of the cyborgs, loomed out from the pavement, admonishing them to move faster.

The kids reached the farther pavement and stood watching the monster return to his original post. Kael noticed, with a smile, that his rump now bore a sparkling advertisement that carried, no doubt, the slogan *Support Autonomy.*

A cop on foot, seeing the sticker, approached the trooper from behind, reached across and tugged it free. As he did so the commando's autonomics over-reacted. The goose flew to his metal hand, and his powered legs brought him around with appalling speed. The cop jumped nervously sideways and slipped to his knees.

Theri laughed.

Con's crew dissolved quickly into the crowd.

Kael made his way through the throng, sidling between two men who were arguing acrimoniously about some matter presumably unconnected with the current proceedings. "...and the child's starting to stutter because of the way you treat him," one of them whined at Kael's face.

"Because of the way *I* treat him? I suppose all that namby-pamby daddy's little lovey...." The other man's petulant voice faded out as Kael and Theri moved on.

The crowd around them turned, thickening and focusing on the steps of the Imperial Monument, now illuminated by the glare of powerful media lasers. The Mayor of Bolte emerged, glazed with the blue of her rain shield.

Her speech of welcome was precisely as vacuous and boring as one might wish. At the moment it tailed off into half-hearted applause, the sound of pipe and drum came from a pirate multi-point source. Heads turned this way and that.

Catsize, dressed in red and black, jester's jingling bells on his masked head, sprang up from the crowd on a floater. His ampli-fied voice, strangely mellow and resonant, announced a modest drama in honor of the Emperor's distinguished envoys.

His floater sank again and he was gone.

A shaft of pure yellow light rose in the midst of the assembly, soft as moonlight in the mist. The dispersed point sources began the Victorian anthem; a number of patriots stiffened their arms in salute. Slurring, the dull melody segued into the heroic strains of the Imperial Anthem, and slurred again into silence.

Someone near Kael grumbled, "Bloody amateurs. Even the bloody Mayor's better than this."

The yellow pillar brightened, and a soughing sigh passed again and again through the crowd. No, wrong on both counts; a tech, or an autonomic intensity regulator, had dimmed the media lasers for a better view of the glowing shaft. And the sound was the sighing, enormously amplified, of a single human being.

Two great black circles had pierced the shaft, gleamingly reflective of the upturned faces of the crowd. Color coalesced about them, larger circles concentric, striated, blue as a placid sea, surrounded by white ovals.

A pair of eyes was regarding the crowd with gentle, maternal acceptance, clear whites veined delicately with a hint of blood vessels, long dark lashes closing and opening gravely once more to behold her children.

For it was a woman's face, not beautiful but warm, tranquil, beneficent: a mother, a madonna. She parted her lips and sang a single note. In the vast hologram field projected above the crowd she rose on her toes, and her tender hands reached to touch the unborn child in her swollen womb.

The plaintive note was taken up by stringed instruments, and carried in an elevation to make the skull vibrate by a chord of electronic tones. Kael found that his eyes had filled with tears; he glanced quickly at Theri, and she squeezed his hand.

The melody emerged—making the muscles of Kael's mouth smile in sudden relief—as a buoyant, jolly kindergarten song. Now the mother lifted her toddler high into the air and spun him around. A hostility toy came into the child's hand; he was older now, a wild haired kid drawing a playful bead on his mom.

There was not a sound from the crowd. New arrivals drifted into vacant spaces, watching the holo. If the official party had thought to move against the scattered pirates, the mood of the assembly held their hand.

The young man, tall and adolescent-wary, stood at his mother's side; as she turned with absent-minded love to kiss him he moved away, and did not see the moment of hurt in her eyes.

A martial note brought briskness to the melancholy melody. Clad in formal military grays, the young man bent over a simulation console, searing imaginary targets with imaginary bolts of stellar radiance.

The holo-drama had shifted to cartoon schema, Kael realized; a brooding element intruded on the sprightly melody, almost subsonically, a merest shading of disquiet. The cartoon soldier stood in blank ennui. The hues had deepened to dull browns and cool blues and grays. All trace of the mother's harmony was leaching from the image.

The soldier dwindled; in his place, an officer reached like an automaton to vid the instructions punched for him by a cadaverous bureaucrat stationed beneath a portrait of the Emperor. The officer took a fax of the message, walked alertly to the soldier, held the words before his face. The soldier dumbly mouthed them to himself. An identical soldier stood at his side, and another behind him, a horde of dehumanized puppets.

The music rose to a hearty, rollicking cadenza for muse; the troops vanished with a sickening lurch into an Aorist Discontinuity.

A disgusted voice muttered near his ear: "The fucking proctors."

Kael took his eyes from the reeling, nauseating mnemonics Catsize had contrived. Con and the redhead were standing beside him. "What?"

"The proctors, they're as dumb as that soldier."

"Some of them aren't too bad," Kael said lamely.

"Come off it. Is your mad friend here?"

"Anla Griffith? Yes, she's here." He felt a pang of tension in his gut. Get on with it, Catsize, they'll cut you off any moment now. You've gone outside the limits of inferential drama, this is blatant statement. Yet the faces around him still stared up at the holo without patriotic outrage, puzzled and locked on.

"Tell her to get properly arrested tonight, will you?"

Kael shuddered slightly. The troops were arrayed in total incineration battle order, running through a scorched place of sagging trees and shattered buildings. A famous patriotic Imperial song from the Estrildinae action on Trantor boomed to the crash of their heavy boots.

He said: "If you wish."

A woman appeared from a flaming doorway, her face hidden by a futile anti-virus mask. The soldier stopped in front of her and took up a defensive stance, laser pointed at her belly. The two figures went to crimson cutout, then frozen black outline in a pitiless white shaft of light. The music stopped utterly.

A poisoned wind whined in the formless rubble. A single plaintive note sang across the crowd; Kael's skin tightened on his cold back, on the soft flesh under his arms.

Full holographic realism exploded back into the field: the woman stumbled forward, the soldier screamed in fear and triggered his weapon. A single searing pulse went into the woman's unprotected belly.

Her clothing puffed and volatilized. Steam gushed from her scorched, perforated womb. She fell in silence.

The trooper stood dully, his face and body abstracting once more to schema. After a moment he knelt beside the fallen woman and carefully removed her virus mask. The woman was his mother.

§

Kael eased his way through the assembly, Theri following. Con and his girl had disappeared as unobtrusively as they had come. A well-known dignitary, caught in the reactivated media lasers and gazing about in confusion, stepped forward to the Monument's podium. His amplified voice fought a losing battle with the babble of the crowd.

The assembly had been virtually mute during the wordless mime; now it seemed that each man caught his neighbor's sleeve and hollered in his ear.

The drizzle eased, and the crowd made it clear that they were impatient with speech-making and baffling holos. The politician bent, murmured to an aide. He stepped down.

Someone gasped. Heads craned. Through the thin, weeping cloud, petals of light unfolded in the night sky. Wind gusted over the Gardens. High above, invisible force fields swept the remaining clouds away. The luminous flowers grew brilliant, prismatic. Beyond Victoria's shadow, stupendous filament fields were being generated from orbit, catching tomorrow's dawn and throwing it ahead in all the shifting hues and glory of official celebration.

Unwatched, the politician was back on his podium. "And when you march, march with joy in the name of your Emperor," he cried to the dazzled crowd.

Kael pushed on, using elbows and knees where necessary, toward the Alliance. He wondered if the politician intended to march and decided he didn't; the "you" had been too well accented, a definite if unconscious stress. The bugger'd be lifted to the Bolte Teleport by official skite.

As Kael reached his friends the crowd started to move, forming into a carnival column ten and fifteen people wide. Children rode the shoulders of adults.

Bad luck, Catsize. A good try, but it'd be hard to whip this lot into insurgent fervor.

Kael reached behind, found Theri's hand, clasped it tightly. The free people of Victoria passed out of the Gardens and gained possession of the old road. A ragged, cheering mass stretched in front of the Alliance and behind it.

The chemical reaction had taken place, the molecules had bonded, and he was now at one with the strolling body of people. And this despite the banality of the evening's agenda, the irrelevance of the whole exercise—even if Anla's covert plans for *agit-prop* destruction came off—to the pain of any infant screaming to death on one of the rebel worlds at whatever monstrous number of degrees Absolute an antipersonnel laser burns.

Water squelched in his shoes. Theri's hair hung in a single tress to the matted fur of her jacket; her face glistened. To their rear Anla and Ben, he noticed, walked arm in arm. Somewhere else in the crowd Con and his action group were doubtless planning mischief. Kael called over his shoulder to Anla:

"My friend Con says to tell you to get properly arrested this time."

"You tell your friend Con to take a running jump at himself."

§

In front of the august stonework of the House of World Assembly, within eyeshot of the Teleport Authority's massive dark premises, the crowd atomized once more. Hot food steamed from scattered portable autovendors, melodiazam infused the air with sentimental mush. Succumbing to the fiesta mood, Ben declared his intention of purchasing them all tubes of floss.

"Don't get lost," his wife warned him in a low voice. "Lonek and Dav are liaising with some of the other resistance groups, we'll be moving in twos and threes out to the edge of the crowd nearest the 'Port."

Tactics and black wind-blown hair: she was lovely, and Ben leaned forward and kissed her mouth. He gave her a parting clip on the rump and pushed off in search of his sticky treat.

Had the legation already arrived? Probably got here days ago, Ben told himself, it's not unknown for long-distance teleporters to come in from the central Archives despite the excruciating expense of fitting them out surgically for the trip. There's an entire hospital embedded in that place, they don't need all the folderol of ambulances and famous medicos standing by. Bloody creepy in any case, getting humped for the voyage, years of biofeedback training to perfect the yoga trance needed to keep you sane.

He remembered the high, cold place. Tachyons follow a duration path at right-angles to relativity time. The elementary tertiary implants fired up the curves and equations into his preconsciousness, facts begging for attention like trained grundles.

It was supposed to be called "humping" because of a mythical beast named the, what was it, the camel, it stored enough food for six months in its hump and all the water it needed in its grotesquely swollen balls. Females of the species must have gone thirsty. Or maybe it was the females who carried half a year's supply of milk in their udders.

What would it feel like to be lugged into the Aorist Closure with a tonne of additional concentrated flab grafted to your torso, air sacs under hideous pressure swelling on your back, dialysis loops turning your piss back into lubrication?

A silly ditty ran through his mind as he bought a bunch of high-pressure floss tubes, greedily squirting a mouthful of pink sugar: de hip-bone connected to da, thigh-bone, de thigh-bone connected to da, knee-bone, de knee-bone connected to da....

"Give me some of that at once, you great guts."

Ben allowed Catsize a tacky bite.

"That was a beautiful advertisement, Catsize. Do you think it'll do any good?"

"If not now, one day, my good Griffith. You must learn to take the long view."

"Try telling Anla that."

A blast of trumpets rang out as Ben passed his tubes around. Magnificent in formal clobber, the Universal Emperor smiled austerely down on them from a grandiose hundred-meter projection.

His shiny black hair decreed a new fashion, clipped straight and clean in line with the tops of his small ears. He had been ruth-stabilized slightly past the full vigor of young manhood, and his brown flat cheeks were etched with faint lines, echoing those at the edges of his dark, epicanthic eyes.

The effect of subtle authority, Ben thought, was vastly more effective than the pseudo-age of Anla's Co-ordinator, bloody old ranting Grey. In his chased, gorgeous armor-of-office, the Lord Lee Sun Chien Shiung was a figure of inconceivable potency.

Prime Speaker Wallechinsky led a standing ovation to the holographic eidetic, the Congress took their places in sight of the crowd and the media pickups, and the Lord Lee faded into the night.

"Where's Catsize gone?" Anla looked swiftly about. "Okay, you and I can start moving now, Ben. Kael, you and Theri stick around for a couple of minutes and follow us. Everyone's gathering for a break to the Teleport, we'll see if this herd follows us when we make our move. See ya."

Wallechinsky's magnified voice was saying, "Latest reports from Central Co-ordination tell us that the Legates have not yet arrived, citizens. Let us begin the presentation of petitions. Rest assured that you will be informed the moment the Emperor's envoys arrive from the Aorist Closure. I now call for the first petition."

Amid a scattering of applause, a burly, ferociously bearded man stepped forward from the front line of the crowd and stood before a visual repeater. His amplified image clarified in front of the Congress.

"To the Parliamentarians of Victoria, greetings from the Arctic Settlers Collective. We humbly petition the people that consideration be given to the establishment of a new power maser in synchronous orbit to provide additional beamed energy to...." The man's bass came in the slightly stilted intonations of one following a peptide prompt. He finished and retreated; a woman from the Attaché's Guild came forward with that body's modest proposal.

It's stupefying, Ben thought. Half these requests have been blocked for the express purpose of allowing them now, magnanimously, as acts of Parliamentary discretion. The other half are harebrained schemes that no one in his right mind would countenance—but giving them an airing here permits the lunatic fringe to bask for an instant in the illusion of momentous contribution to the commonweal.

He gave a gasp of laughter, which sneezed pink floss over a surprised child, as a spokesperson for the Autonomous Aerial

Objects Skywatch craved funding to track down the alien spacecraft and their gray crew that were haunting the galaxy, as the conspiracy of bureaucrats knew only too well. The fellow seemed set to launch a detailed exposition of his case when the repeater shifted deftly to a woman from the Bookmakers' Union.

Anla nudged him, glancing up from her library.

"They've arrived. One of the South glacier Teleports."

"That'll disappoint the sightseers. Standing in the rain half the night and they'd have been better off at home in front of their hollies."

"If they're cross enough, we might be able to get them to follow us."

For a quarter of an hour, no further announcement was forthcoming, Ben licked the last of his floss from his moustache and placed the spent tube in a disposal. The crowd stirred restlessly; enough of them had been checking their libraries for the word to get around. The Prime Speaker's face flashed into existence above them.

"Fellow citizens, good news!" Yells and stamping feet. "The Legates have arrived, and bear news that will cheer us all. We shall return to the declaration of petitions in a few minutes. First, I have the great honor of announcing a message to the people of Victoria from His Majesty."

Trumpets blared again, and some of those squatting on their heels stood up. "On your feet, you fuckwits," Anla hissed to several diehards. "Do you want to attract attention?"

Ben gazed about in gloomy boredom. The moment was gone, if it had ever put in an appearance. Half listening, he learned that His Supreme Majesty was (1) in spiffing good health, both of mind and body, (2) the parent of certain additional children, and (3) contesting the next election—surprise, surprise—to the Imperial Throne. Not one to stand down politely at the end of ten terms, old father Lee.

Something caught his attention; he looked up at the holographs of the three Legates. In the congealed seconds that followed he stared at the robust portraits: the heavy Slavic cheeks of Olaf Basov, the hooded, mahogany eyes of Trofim Buist, the broad, pore-pitted nose of Marie Wang Dawson.

From somewhere near at hand came the electrifying scream of someone's awful premonition.

"...that ninety-three years ago those responsible for the treasonous insurrection mounted a total internal blockage on the planet's Teleport loci. Despite repeated pleas from His Majesty, the rebel leaders refused to relinquish their illegal seizure of Imperial property and command-posts. Troops dispatched to restore order were poisoned as they emerged helpless and unarmed within the illicitly-occupied munitions fortresses. Imperial authorities were dispossessed and ousted by the criminal regime, and carried the news of an entire planetary population in revolt against His Majesty."

Anla's fingers pressed Ben's to the bone; they stared at one another with the gaze of the dead.

"Accordingly, on July 4, 3921, His Majesty ordered the launching from the nearest Regional Armory of a relativistic warship bearing two photospheric disrupters."

The man standing in front of Ben started to cry; the child in his arms, uncomprehending, began to wail as well.

"The population was informed of their sentence two months before star-zero, and invited to abandon their blockade. They refused. Apparently an attempt was made to divert an asteroid into the trajectory of the warship; the attempt failed. Even then, less than ten percent of the insurgent population chose to enter the Aorist Closure. Most of these had small infants with them, and have been remanded in custody."

The Prime Speaker was silent for a moment. His huge image stared down at the crowd, flanked by the faces of the Legates. He smiled as he said:

"You will be pleased and relieved to hear that this intolerable threat to His Majesty's authority is now at an end. Sixteen days ago, I'm sorry, uh, thirty-one days ago, the star NGC 621-upsilon 904 was triggered to nova. The planet Chomsky, and its intransigent rebels, no longer exists."

A light wind shook the leaves of a nearby tree. Ben felt his legs tremble slightly, and the inside of his cheek was bleeding. In the mighty trumpet fanfare, he thought he heard delayed screams and cries, but the brazen sound echoed and re-echoed in overwhelming triumph.

He had turned with Anla toward the Teleport buildings, was running in tear-blinded savage fury to rend and destroy, when he realized that the monstrous sound behind him was not electronic stridency, not the crashing of an impossible surf. He stumbled, half-incredulous, his throat working, and turned back again.

Most of the assembly was a blur of jerky motion, jumping up and down, their hands coming together before their faces with a roar of triumph. They were applauding the death of the uppity anarchists' world.

§

The autonomist fragment of the assembly raged in the glistening black and yellow night toward the symbol of murder.

Kael felt a weird clinical detachment. Is this grief we're riding?.

His own cheeks were dry, though Theri's ran with tears.

I have never known anyone from Chomsky, he realized. It has always been a place of abstracts: charged with distant hopes, yes, an archetype of the impossible-made-flesh, a symbol, but not a neighborhood one has walked.

The news embargo had been almost total. Hardly a face one could summon from eidetics, and those dredged up from sources old a millennium ago. Hardly a name one would recognize. Our grief, if that is what it is, has an impersonal quality.

Chomsky has gone. He tried to get the fact down out of his cortex and into his nerves, his endocrine centers.

The air in his immediate vicinity stank with fury and fear. Library reports flickered at light-speed in the moving web of the human-slow ranks. Voices shouted, ran together.

"They've barricaded the way to the Teleport."

The vanguard slowed, allowing the column to bunch up. Oxygen-debt, Kael noted to himself, and the thought was ludicrously apt to his floating mood. His lungs pumped, and his muscles began to feel the pace they'd been sustaining.

"They want us to do this," he said to Theri. It was hard to speak. She gave him a look of stoned bewilderment. "There was absolutely no reason to tell us about Chomsky at that point." Somehow it was important to keep talking, to work this out. "It was a provocation. They must *know*—"

The rows had thickened to twenty or more.

Someone shouted, "Link arms!"

How many are we? Five hundred? Not much more. Those fucking bastards were *cheering*.

Theri, at his left, slid her arm through his, and a heavily muscled man locked himself to his other side. The tightly knit human block started to rotate on one corner, swinging slowly into the square fronting the Teleport Authority.

Forty or fifty light years. Nearly a century in transit, the extinction of a solar system in the bowels of a splinter of steel.

The long view: Catsize and the Empire both. You could see the hideous logic of it. Let one world through the gap into freedom and that world could build starsmashers of its own. If you stop Imperial guerrillas from getting in through the Aorist system, it's hard to get out yourself and there's not much you can do at the far end, naked and frail. But if you have the industrial capacity and the freedom to use it, you can terrorize any world in reach of near-light-speed delivery. Even without nova igniters, the punitive ship was itself a relativistic bomb carrying enough kinetic energy to smash a world as it slammed in from the depths of night.

Blue and orange burnt the sky: police reinforcements fell into the square, lining up behind and alongside the marching rebels. Kael shuffled on, held firmly by his mistress and the manual toiler.

They went forward now in a sacred hush—no weeping, no chanting, no angry songs of resistance, just the shuffling of wet feet and the clash of steel commando boots.

Kael shivered as an angry murmur rolled from the front of the column. A hundred meters before the empty Teleport lobby a barricade of sullen red light lay across the ground. What are they doing with innocent incoming voyagers, he wondered, arriving all unknowing, from the stars and galaxies fading into the billion light-year darkness behind those gathering clouds? Taking them out through the emergency tunnels, or giving them free buzz and pleading emergency?

Reports came in from the other side of the immense building. The organizers had their intelligence network nicely set up in advance. Not unexpectedly, a similar line of defense protected the Teleport from a feinting attack in the reciprocal direction. Within this ring of glowing force-fields a solid body of police and armored skites waited silently.

Kael felt the rising tension of the group; his arms were tugged in their sockets by its physical expression. Without turning his head, he sensed the police closing in from behind, sealing the trap.

From the roof of the hotel opposite a blast of light smashed through the renewed rain onto the sea of heads. A billion spectators, sitting before their hollies, were about to get an unprecedented chance to test their wits as realtime strategists in the warmth and dryness of their own homes, to choose their teams for the coming tournament, relayed live from the arena.

How many would be mourning Chomsky? None of them had conscripted relatives there; that was one blessing, Kael thought bitterly, in sanitizing an internally blockaded world.

He peered between the heads of the front lines at the grim power-wall and the blue-flickering line fixed shoulder to shoulder behind it. Why are they doing it this way, he asked himself, why are they making it a brute contest of muscle and bone? Whatever we do, he thought in sudden piercing despair, we cannot escape the realization that they have modeled our options in advance, to the last memetic detail, and prodded us to their own ultimate profit.

In the Newstralian surf, last summer, knowing he had caught a bad wave and having forsaken the moment of grace when the swimmer can pull out, Kael had seen, from its surging crest, the inevitability of the dump onto the hard sea floor. Locked in tight, now, to this slow human wave about to spend itself in a splatter of scorching sparks, Kael felt in his stomach the unavoidable, fore-ordained crash.

We must mourn them, but it is too late to help them; we must carry their lives into our own, not to our deaths. What expiation can we win if we bring the beating down upon our own bodies?

He looked sideways at Theri. Arms enmeshed in the human chain, she stood with hands clasped in front of her, responsive to the electric tug and surge of the crowd, the justified cohesion of the multitude. He himself felt none of it. The chemical bond had been false, a mere accident of contiguity; the truth of the matter was that he wanted to go home.

The front line of the block came abreast of the barriers. Pressure from behind built up quickly, the grip on his arms tightened; a sonic grenade exploded a few meters ahead, sending Kael to his knees. He came close to whimpering, totally trapped.

Smog bombs ignited in the front lines. The media lasers from the hotel roof turned the smog and rain to a dancing, golden haze.

An immense lace of sparks flung upward triumphantly and a section of the field died, countermanded by some electronics genius. Little Con? The pressure from the line of bodies in front of his own suddenly vanished and Kael was flung and dragged forward.

With a hoarse cheer the human tide surged through the gap. Theri tripped, swung like an infant from the arms of Kael and her other companions, regained her balance.

Swearing cops ran in from the flanks, trying to stem the flood by hand. No energy weapons had yet been fired. A cyborg soared out of the smog, the lasers catching his cruel metal features. It was theater, really, nothing more.

Kael staggered, found himself free of clinging arms, and waited alone for the rapidly clearing smog to reveal the state of play.

§

Catsize, in fugue, ran.

I am the shadow of the waxwing slain

Ah, Vladeema, dead yourself these twenty centuries and more, you would not have relished the planet Chomsky. A stinking hot world at the best, under its fat white star. Few enough peaks there of alpine crisp, and no lucerne for the melting snow. 0 my prophetic soul. The bolt of stellar incandescence, human steam smoking from her womb. They were my friends and now they have gone away.

He found, within his ancient mind, a place to hide. It was a corner of concealment where he'd dallied before, treading the boards for his solitary amusement. His mood of voiceless, uncoupled desolation spangled in the momentary vision of the wild throng lifting their faces to the flaring light and bursting into song, police and anarchists joining hands in long, high-stepping chorus lines. Color by technicolor; lyrics, Gilbert and Sullivan.

§

Some two hundred men and women, Kael estimated, had managed to break through into defended territory and now clustered noisily twenty meters from the hastily reactivated barrier.

To their left the Teleport lobby lay exposed, protected only by a thin line of police. Van and riot skites were drawn up at the top end of the corral; others hovered overhead, hard-edged clouds of death.

A tight-lipped man in civilian clothes up ahead quickly assembled a detachment to contain and expel the infiltrators, slapping all the while a pair of leather gloves, monotonously, into the palm of one hand.

A voice cried hoarsely: "Forward to the Teleport!"

No one moved.

The closing semi-circle of police encountered the infiltrators. Commandos were being held in reserve. A few people lay down. A cop trod on one outstretched hand. Voices yelped in outrage, and whistles blew.

A scuffle broke out at the edge; half a dozen conscript cops plunged in, dragging a child of Con's age into the open. The boy struggled like a newly landed fish, twisting and kicking in the net of black arms. His jacket rode up over his head, and ripped. The white skin of his back and midriff increased his resemblance to a struggling fish. A police van skimmed quickly towards the tussle. From behind the force-fields, the main group's angry jeers filled the square.

"Murderers!"

"Cretinous slaves!"

"Pick on someone your own size, why don't yer?"

The cops tried to stuff the boy into the open hold of the van; he caught hold of the roof and held himself out. A commando stepped forward and delicately laid the edge of his goose on the boy's wrist. The boy let go with a jerk and crashed into the van. First arrest of the night.

Kael listened to the hoots of the crowd on the far side of the barrier. The infiltrators remained silent, watching the circle of police. Kael looked at the cops' faces: the hate and joy of body-to-body violence was starting to bring out a nervous arrogance. He looked at his companions: alight with the holy flame of battle. He felt the utter weariness of the prophet in his stomach.

On the vulnerable edge of the herded group, Theri was confronting a solid wall of advancing force-fields. She stood firm, obstinate. The field tumbled her, fragmented into whipping web, and Theri was snatched from the increasing anger of the crowd.

Lasers swung onto the scene and Kael watched his woman

being levitated to a waiting van, her face—white in the blazing column of light—mouthing unheard words of scorn. Second arrest of the night.

Why are they letting it go on like this? The bastards could tie us all up in tanglefields any time they feel like it.

Kael turned and with deliberate steps crossed the space between the infiltrators and the energy walls, confronting the line of cops.

"I want to pass through."

"That's what you think."

Kael wondered if the cop were as old as some of the kids in pre-graduate. An apprentice from a Cop Clan by the look of him, nervous and very pale. The blinding monochrome from the hotel smashed over Kael's shoulders, making the cop blink. Am auditory bug fell from the darkness like an inquisitive bird and hovered above their heads, deploying its sensors.

"You realize we are now on realtime holovision?"

An older cop took charge:

"What's yer code?"

Kael regarded him politely.

"Are you arresting me for a specific offence? Peaceful assembly is not a crime, and you have not seen me act violently, I think."

"Give me yer library I said."

The bug spun in the shocking light: not a bird, a small spider hanging from an invisible thread. Kael shrugged and handed over his library. The senior cop pulsed his code to a van library and handed it back.

"Let him through."

Kael passed through the line of police and the dull red bars of the field went off for an instant as he crossed the barricade. The shaft of light swung away to a more dynamic confrontation somewhere else in the field of play. Something brutal struck Kael in the back, spun him on his knees in the crowd.

After a dazed interval he got back to his feet; his hands were slimy. A head was outlined against the police van's translucent shield, but glare and distance made it impossible to tell if it were Theri or the young boy. The expeditionary force was being driven back at a steady rate toward the place he'd just crossed. Cyborg quirts added a measure of agony to the pushing control fields.

Two more arrests were made. No nauseating aerosols, sonics, broadband sensory disrupters, certainly no lethal lasers. This was nonchalant terror. Infants getting a touch of approved negative reinforcement.

The retreating anarchists and their sympathizers reached the barriers. Red bars faded to let them through. The crowd around Kael surged forward involuntarily into the gap and met greater pressure from the herded, exiting infiltrators.

A man's body, floppy in unconsciousness, was forced into the air like driftwood. There was blood on the face of a girl. All cyborgs had their gooses out: skinny egg-plants, pain, for the infliction of.

Kael allowed himself to be pushed around in the crowd until the last radical was expelled from the cops' chosen territory.

Mocking lights came on in the Teleport lobby, and blobby faces peered out into the pouring night. The pressures of the crowd eased and Kael watched passively while the van containing Theri and the others rose into the air. Its lift-coil pulsed obscenely.

§

Ben wandered aimlessly through the milling crowd. Two children passed him, walking away hand in hand from the contained riot. The boy bent down and picked up a sodden Chomsky flag which he hung reverently over his shoulder.

A cruising police skite dropped in front of the couple, blocking their path. Three cops got out, ripped the flag from the boy, kneed him in the balls, threw his doubled-up figure into the skite, and got back in. They appeared to be interviewing him in the back with many gesticulations.

The girl stood amid the thinning crowd in an attitude of hysterical amazement. Intensified rain hissed over her in fine, curving sheets. She continued shakily across the square, pawing helplessly at her face.

Ben opened his throat and screamed in rage, running at the slowly levitating cop skite. His boots clanged on metal and plast as he found leverage and hauled himself to its dripping roof.

The square tilted and fell away dizzyingly; he grappled himself to the roof sensors and began kicking the skite's glo-panels into fluorescent shards. Pieces fell into the night like lonely fireflies.

From the media emplacements a shaft of dazzling laser light swept his jerking, spread-eagled form as the skite dropped again toward the sodden earth.

§

A man's hand fell on Anla's arm. She crouched and spun swiftly:

"Oh shit, Jard, I thought you were the fuzz. I'm surprised to see you here. Come to make a parliamentary petition?"

"They've saturated the holly with this thing. I'm an observer for the Committee on Violations of Citizen Rights."

"Observed any juicy violations?"

"Very funny, Anla, it's impossible."

"Really? What a shame the cops don't wear luminous placards with their codes in big Eezy-Reed numerals."

"They've jammed my library and smashed two of our pickups."

"It's a nasty scene, Jard."

"It's not only the cops either."

"No discipline in the ranks?"

"Half these people are just babies, they've never been Millioned to a frontier world, never known anything but urban affluence. Class analysis, Anla. It's easy to yell at the cops, but the police and the militia are the ones who are most likely to be sent off to die if our masters decide to double the troops on

Kurd, say. This lot haven't a clue who the real enemy is."

"But it was different when the cops attacked the anarchists on Trantor?"

"That was a structured revolution, not an emotional outburst."

"A really good point, Jard; let's just give thanks that this sort of miscalculation won't happen on Chomsky, at any rate."

Jard started to reply, but the crowd gave a sudden surge and the two clones were pushed clumsily backwards.

A man darted through the crowd, keeping his head down and ducking from side to side, almost swimming. It was futile: the side of his face glowed where a cop had printed him with a signal emitter. He passed quickly between Anla and Jard and disappeared, if only from sight, into the closing ranks. Two commandos shouldered their way inexorably after him, barging through the obstructing mass of people. A woman stood insanely obstinate in their path, turning her back against their onslaught. One of the cyborgs stopped and arrested her. He dragged her off backwards while his colleague continued his juggernaut pursuit.

The woman struggled, kicking out with her feet; the crowd booed; Jard began to follow them as rapidly as the crowd would allow. The augmented trooper vaulted the main crush and dragged the woman across a relatively open space to a waiting van.

Jard caught up and started to speak to him. There was no response. Jard put a hesitant, restraining hand on the massive steel arm. The commando whirled, swearing, and lashed out with one powered arm, striking Jard on the chest.

Anla saw death in Jard's white face as he fell back, his hand spread against his neat bureaucrat-style coat. He started to sink to his knees.

Desperate and efficient, Anla parted the crowd with her shoulders, the breath pent in her lungs.

Three cops from the waiting van beat her to him: two took an arm apiece while the third brought up the rear, a hand clutching Jard's ruff. He was loaded quickly into the hold of the van, his head turning as the locking fields caught him. The blood was draining back into his face. He was still trying to say something calm and rational to the arresting cops.

Anla stopped. She took a number of deep breaths and watched the van lift away. Somewhere a siren was wailing.

§

Catsize the Red Guard stood in the icy streets of St Petersburg.

Behind the bright windows of the Winter Palace the besieged provisional government sat and doodled, dispatching vain telegraph messages into the rising fury. Kerensky gone, the day of the counterrevolutionary was all but spent. All power to the Soviets!

The workers and poor peasants were on the march. From the endless steppes of East Bolte, from the frozen rivers of Bjelke, from the wolf-haunted forests of El Cheapo Street on Newstralia, from the dark factories and mills of a billion worlds, the downtrodden, oppressed and starving masses were rising.

Behind his back the yunkers and Cossacks tore at the people, arrogant and superseded by history, the light taking their bloody sabers.

A Cossack thrust into the crowd, knocking a buxom peasant girl to the ground. The masses redoubled their struggles, anger in their rough proletarian cries. An extraordinarily thin woman fell against the Red Guard, distraught and choking with dialectical fervor. The chatter of machine-gun fire split the air and mingled the fumes of spent powder with the snow-laden air.

The gaunt woman clutched at the sturdy Red Guard beside her, rain running down her face, strands of gray hair lying limp across the lines of her forehead. Catsize felt his heart lurch. She was old, physiologically old.

"It is happening all over...they took away our ruth and locked us in and let us die...forty years, eating from our own filth... plantation-overseers with the dogs—"

"Huh? Madam, you're on the wrong set."

The anti-personnel whine of a police skite sounded briefly some distance overhead. Even at that remove Catsize felt his brain cringe in his skull. The whine cut off abruptly. Wrong switch.

A youth nursing a dangling arm made his way gingerly through the crowd toward the empty spaces of the public drop-space. The woman muttered to herself in a language Catsize could not understand. She turned to him again:

"The wire and the sky...slavemasters...my husbands and my children...they took the children separately...all over again."

Christ on crutches, this woman must be nearly as old as me. Outright slavery was abolished in the twenty-third century.

Catsize put a soaking arm around the woman's shoulders; she was exactly his height. He led her trembling away, picking the shortest possible route through the fragmented groups. Her shoulders were incredibly thin under his arm.

"It's all right, it's all right, it's not happening again. There aren't any plantations now. This is Victoria. It's just a lot of kids having a night out. Worse things happen at the football. It can't happen here."

Catsize took his charge away from the melee, into the black reaches of the night. The woman became quieter, but she shivered every few seconds and continued to mutter to herself.

"Where do you live?"

The woman moaned.

"Hey! Where do you live?"

"In the slaves' dome, by the north gate."

"Now, mother. Where do you live now?"

The woman shook her head, muttering again.

He sized her up. "Do you live in Gandhi?"

The name registered:

"Yes, it is in the Gandhi ziggurat that I live."

"Good, it's not far, we can walk if we have to but I'll try for a hitch."

He freed one hand and pulled out his library. No, commuter corridors would have been diverted—try a public cab. He held her tight against him, waiting patiently.

Eventually, one of the bright bubbles fell and hovered beside them. The autonomics were none too happy at having the cab's seats dripped on, but grudgingly took them away.

§

Anla emerged from the masses, water streaming down her face.

"The whole bloody thing's turned to chaos, there's not a hope of getting to the Teleport now. They've forgotten Chomsky, it's just turned into an anti-cop festival."

"What did you expect, Anla, a full-scale autonomist uprising?"

"Don't be dull, Kael. Where's Theri?"

"Arrested."

"So's Ben. Silly bugger went for a ride on the roof of a cop skite. They've got Jard too."

"I know." Kael looked up from the screen of his library. "I've got a list of those arrested, but it doesn't show the charges. And I can't raise Theri."

"Of course you can't, the first thing they do is take your library away. I wonder what they'll charge Jard with."

"Assault and battery probably."

"That'll fix the old loon—he came here asking to be violated. Let's go, the rain's getting worse and the action boring."

"Where to?"

"Home, of course, unless you can think of anywhere better."

Kael followed, as Anla walked quickly through the crowd, wishing he shared her unconcern. They cleared the last tatters of the exhausted riot; Anla lifted an authoritative arm, bleep in hand, commanding one of a bunch of low-hovering public cabs to stop. One did, immediately.

§

In the steamed-up cabin, Kael punched the codes of a dozen police stations. None of the autonomic reply circuits offered any additional information. The pointlessness of the exercise irritated Anla, it was like a nervous tic.

"Will you put that thing away?"

"There must be something we can do."

"Look, Kael, your sweet little Theri has got herself arrested along with ten dozen others. A night in the cells, that's all, won't do her any harm, and even if we did find out precisely where they're being held their cases probably won't be heard till three in the morning. And if it's any consolation to you, they're supposed to be allowed one call, so she'll reach you wherever you are. Stop clucking like an anxious parent."

To her exasperation, he just slumped in the corner of the cab. Anla roughly took his hand. They flew, unspeaking, through the dreary, rain-filled night to the Griffith dwelling. Looking sideways at Kael she felt a strong desire to hit him over the head with something solid, but found him sexy, even in the depths of his doleful undramatic depression—like a half-drowned Greek god playing Hamlet.

§

Toasting his bare toes, Kael gloomily watched the spot-heater's glowing plasma. Anla brought him coffee laced with buzz-dust.

She had changed, he saw, into a forest green jump-suit with a silver belt. She sat on the hand-woven rug beside him and started to dry her hair, leaning forward and letting it hang in a heavy black veil over her face. Drops of water from her brush hissed into the magnetic field.

"Look, a night of detention will do her nothing but good."

"She's probably being roughed up by a lot of thuggy fuzz."

"Balls. She's probably singing jolly songs of sedition with her cell-mates." After a moment Anla added, "Anyway, it's what she wanted. If she hadn't wanted to get arrested she needn't have, and if you'd wanted to be with her you could have got yourself arrested as well."

"Not out here in the dominions, Anla, they segregate the sexes."

Anla put her hand to Kael's face, her long, cool fingers blotting out the plasma glare. He held her to himself, his hands stroking her back and neck, the drying mass of her hair against his cheek. Oh hold me, Anla petal. Anla laughed, the warmth of her body hard against Kael. She kissed him with a firm insistent mouth, seeking his tongue with hers. Anla, Anla, I can't fuck you now, not with any joy or love, don't try and make me. Unhurried and well-versed, Anla found his prick. She held her head back, her eyes on his with a mocking need. Kael resisted.

"Charioteers, Kael, you're not being all faithful to Theri, are you?"

"Yes, in a way, and to Ben."

"Bloody hell."

"He's my friend and it hurts him when you screw around."

"Your trouble, Sir Pureheart, is that basically you're scared, scared as a general policy. Where's your autonomist affirmation?"

"Rhubarb to you, kid."

"Well yes, Socrates, deep inside I've no doubt you're more aggressive than the lot of us, you just repress it more effectively. What sort of fantasies do you have, Kael?"

"I trust this excellent bit of therapy is charged to Medbank."

"Not at all, you're going to have to pay for it personally."

Anla neatly rolled Kael to the floor. In the silent struggle Kael, by virtue of his strength, gained the advantage. He sat astride Anla, holding her shoulders to the rug. Anla relaxed, perfectly at ease in defeat.

Her hair lay black on the rug's black and red. The dark green of her jump-suit opened in a long, sharp triangle at her throat. Her skin was smooth and olive brown, even in winter. Happily, submissively, she smiled up at Kael. He relaxed his hold. "Look, Anla, it's not that—"

With an animal deftness she caught him around the neck with her left leg and bent him violently backwards. He thought she had broken his windpipe. Anla sat over him, dominant. Kael, totally limp, closed his eyes and turned away from the plasma glare centimeters from his forehead.

Anla sat looking down at him for a few seconds. Putting a hand to his chin, she turned his face to hers, bent forward with a sigh and kissed him gently. She rose and walked to the door.

"Sorry, Kael petal, I'll race you off some other time."

§

Theri, Ben and Jard, at liberty, sat drinking and eating nutrients rudimentary but welcomingly hot with their comrades of the night. Through Lonek's kitchen wove a varying number of people, recounting grievances, adding their own judicial sentences to the sundry tally: obstruction, resisting arrest, seditious or indecent language, disturbing the peace. News came of arbitrary "leaders" being held in the city for incitement to riot and riotous assembly, and one unheard charge of malicious wounding.

Jard et al had been convicted and let out at 0400, Theri with bruises on her arm, Ben with a piratical black eye, into the custody of a deputation from Jard's Committee.

Someone switched Lonek's holly to an early 'cast of the morning news. Grim media faces spoke of Riot During Petition Assembly, and of Anarchy At The Teleport. Miniaturized scuffles reprised in the holly comer: figures trapped by dull red force-walls, cowering in confused huddles, cops hurling back anarchists, arrests.

The room cheered in good humored derision at night-flying Ben, flailing at the cop skite.

An earnest editorialist faced the gathering:

"When a minority of citizens on a democratic world tries to force its views on others by disrupting the civil order, that minority can succeed only in imperiling our Imperial privileges, and encouraging the rabble element that...."

Lonek bared his teeth savagely:

"Meanwhile back on a cinder called Chomsky—"

§

Kael paced around his apt, a somber inhospitable hulk anchored in a cold inhospitable city. His own spotplasma gave out its beam of directional heat, toasting the skin and leaving the bones to freeze. He looked at his library: 0711. An absurdly early hour to be awake.

He walked to the cold-field. It contained an uninviting collection of bits and pieces. He took out an opened foil of milk and a scowl egg. A thin film of half dried milk clung to the upper half of the foil. Kael drank it and seared the egg, setting the timer at random. He looked out into the dismal morning light. He felt foolish and hungry. It had been a bad night: visions of Theri fighting the fuzz; of Anla, tall and laughing.

Part of the white was still a liquid translucent blob. He ate the tepid thing in three quick bites as the door opened.

Radiant, happy Theri clattered in.

"Hello, love, just been convicted for offensive behavior. Shit, the cops are creeps."

Kael watched his mistress, her hair tangled and knotted, a flush on her face, squatting in front of the plasma warming her hands.

"Ben went for obstruction and damage," she told him cheerfully. "Have you watched the news?"

"Briefly."

"They showed Mart and Ris being arrested."

"Really."

"What's the matter with you?"

"Nothing."

"You don't seem too happy. We're planning a lightning raid on the Teleport now they've removed the force-fields. Roar overhead in a couple of skites with the cybernet repeaters suppressed—Con says he can fix it to last thirty seconds—pelt the place with grenades, and roar away. Going to come?"

"No."

"Don't be so bloody dreary." She foraged for something to eat.

Kael sat in a chair, and thought about memetic hypercycles capable of predicting the mass movements of an octillion human beings. He looked at Theri: alive and happy in the revolutionary morning, hot from the fray and in the mood for more, the fire of purpose in her veins, the warmth of comradeship in her words.

"I don't think you ought to go."

"Why the fuck not?"

"Because there's no point in it and you'll probably be arrested again."

"Oh, fucking Chariots, Kael, just because you're so pissweak there's no need for everybody else to be." Theri, contemptuous, turned on Kael, slumped in his chair about to speak, and fore-stalled him: "I know exactly what you're going to say, Kael. You're going to say that rattling the Teleport windows with grenades won't do anything to put Chomsky back. You'll prob-ably say we're father-fixated with the authorities."

"Something like that."

"Well, I'm just not interested."

Theri stood up quickly from the table, pushing the plate away, and left the room. Kael continued his study of plasma heaters.

They were said to be more resources-conservative than central heating, a feature admired in energy mechanisms by Catsize. The poet had held on more than one occasion that despite the methane reserves locked up in the gas giants the universe was finally on the verge of fucking itself. The spot-heater Kael and Theri rented was altogether a classier job than Anla's and Ben's, with two separate magnetic bottles, one for each of the plasmas, providing the potential for a lewd, flushed-cheek buttock effect. But then, only one of the plasmas was actually operative these days, which was a point against it.

In the bathroom, Theri was singing above the shower's hiss.

§

The poet kicked brutally at the rabid thornglee as he picked his way to the Cathouse. Coming down. Soon he would weep. When your rooster crows at the break of dawn

He closed the door, activated his library. He brooded for a time, and started to enter a poem into temporary store. Once he giggled. Goodbye, Smeeth. Groaning at what he saw on the display, he started a second stanza:

> God's umbreller is made of air
> keeps the nasty vacuum out.
> God, it's said, has air to spare
> enables us all to sing & shout.
> One fine day in the winedark spaces
> between the stars where god's hidden face is
> the Charioteers got restless
> left with a space-hiss
> bumped into god
> upset his umbreller.
> Space poured in like coal to a cellar.

The final stanza was worse. It was evident even to Catsize that he was hysterical with grief. He beamed. It was a terrible poem. At the end he keyed:

For services rendered

Catsize added the name Smeeth knew him by. He accessed Smeeth's work code, mailed the poem to the office system of his patron. He switched off the library and lay down on his bed. On the road again. Nowhere to go. No vengeance, no saving fantasy, no faith, no hope, no caritas. He had owned these gifts for a thousand years but when he turned about they had gone. And for another thousand he had possessed despair merely.

I met a young girl, she gave me a rainbow

Tears began to leak from his meshed lashes.

Then I'll stand on the ocean until I start sinkin'

...Plangent, ancient, angry dirge, like a voided promise of flame.

ABOUT THE AUTHORS

Damien Broderick is an award-winning Australian science fiction writer, editor and critical theorist, with a Ph.D. from Deakin University. Formerly a senior fellow in the School of Culture and Communication at the University of Melbourne, he currently lives in San Antonio, Texas. He has written or edited some 60 books. His 1980 novel *The Dreaming Dragons* (revised in 2009 as *The Dreaming*) is listed in David Pringle's *Science Fiction: The 100 Best Novels*—and with Paul Di Filippo, he has published a sequel to Pringle's book, *Science Fiction: The 101 Best Novels, 1985-2010*. *Post Mortal Syndrome*, written with his wife Barbara Lamar, was serialized online by *Cosmos* science magazine, and later published by Borgo Press in the USA. His recent short story collections are *Uncle Bones*, *The Qualia Engine*, and *Adrift in the Noösphere*. In 2013, he collaborated with Grand Master Robert Silverberg on the novel *Beyond the Doors of Death*.

Rory Barnes has written six novels with Broderick, beginning with *Valencies* and most recently their short novel *Human's Burden*. A widower with two adult sons, he lives in Adelaide, Australia. He has also written the novels *The Bomb-Monger's Daughter*, *Water from the Moon* (with James Birrell), the very funny Horsehead trilogy for young readers, *Night Vision* and *The Dragon Raft* for young adults, and *Space Junk*, a futuristic novel inspired by the saga of the Asian refugee boat people imprisoned or turned away by the Australian government.